A

No where to run ...

Lifetime
to Wait

THE DARKEST SERIES

Jackie Mae

Cover design by, Carolyn Sheltraw
Edited by, Ashton Farmanara

ISBN-13: 978-0-9916149-2-9 (paperback) /
978-0-9916149-3-6 (ebook)

Printed in the United States of America

To,

My husband, always my knight

And a special thanks to,

Larry and Rebecca for being the best

And to,

Richard, whose love and support
has meant so much

A Note from Jackie Mae:

Welcome. Come along with me to a place where the Ones walk amongst us. Where ordinary people, like you and I, have hidden strengths. When all else fails, the meek shall not be mild, but bold and daring.

THE ONES (The Darkest Series) is the first book. A LIFETIME TO WAIT (The Darkest Series) is the next installment in the series.

I hope all my readers will enjoy the ride.

Contents

Chapter 1

He came out of nowhere, tackling her to the ground like a battering ram, milliseconds before she felt the heat from the beam of light. It had just missed them. Thankfully, he had rolled them to the right. Jerking her up by her shirt, he pulled her along to the edge of the forest. Wedged between him and a large Sycamore tree, she barely had time to look at his face, when the tree was hit with such force a large portion of its top half exploded and came raining down. He took her hand and ran through the forest.

Sprinting farther into the interior, he abruptly turned sharply to his left and ran at break-neck speed for the riverbank. Her heart was pounding; she was finding it difficult to understand the events unfolding before her. Running over tree roots and rocks, the man was unknowing or uncaring that she would falter any second now and they would both go tumbling over the rocky trail. She knew she couldn't keep up this pace. As if somehow knowing what she was thinking, he stopped for a moment. Out of breath, she leaned over putting both hands on her knees for support. She began contemplating what exactly was going on, when he pulled her forward slowly. She was rudely awakened from her thoughts when the ice cold water hit her senses.

"Here Brooke, take this, hurry."

He handed her a reed. She grabbed the reed and took a life-saving deep breath a mere moment before he shoved her face underwater. He squeezed in close to her and none-too-gently pushed her up against the embankment. The cold was slowly seeping into her pores and making her brain foggy.

She wasn't sure if she was still holding up the reed when he took her hand. She could hear voices calling her name, over and over again. She started to stir when the man beside her held her tightly, shook her just enough to help her focus. She couldn't see anything, but the voices were near. She felt the coiled tension in him.

Minutes or maybe hours went by before he hauled her up and out of the murky water. She lay motionless in the grass, welcoming the sun's rays pouring over her body. She began to shake uncontrollably. He leaned over her, murmured in her ear that she would be alright, that he would take care of her. She sure hoped he was one of the good guys, because she was fading into unconsciousness fast.

She awoke to the smell of herbs and spices all around her. She smelled some other heavenly aroma coming from down the hall. Perhaps her host had cooked a meal. She sat up and slowly looked around. As she looked around, she saw she was in a man's room. It had masculine hues with little pops of color. She suddenly shivered from a breeze upon her shoulders. It was then she looked down, realizing she had on a man's shirt and little else. *Where am I? What's going on here?* The implications were overwhelming. Lying back down for a moment she inhaled her pillow. It smelled manly. She liked it.

"Brooke, if you're hungry, food is on the table," called a man's voice from down the hall.

She did not respond. Truth be told, she was terrified in that moment.

He added, "If you prefer to shower first, your clothes are laid out in the bathroom."

She quickly walked to the bathroom and saw her clothes were clean and fresh towels were draped over a chair. The bathroom itself looked big enough to be the size of some apartments in New York City. The frameless glass door led to a four person sized tiled shower enclosure with eight body jets. Even the toilet was unbelievable. It had a panel on the side of it with multiple selections available. *How many features did a toilet need to have?* she wondered. She locked the door and took a luxurious shower. Using all the body jets, she let the water wash over her. The tension slowly washed away, easing her many aches and pains, and she thoroughly enjoyed herself. She took her time dressing and blow drying her hair. She found a mini hairbrush on the counter and helped herself.

She was afraid to open the door. Who was this man? What was the intent? Who had undressed her? How had she arrived here? And where was here? So many questions, enough stalling. Besides, she needed to eat, as she was beginning to feel light-headed.

She opened the door. In the doorway stood a man that was formidable looking and really, really strong. She had serious thoughts about closing the door and locking it again.

Then, he smiled at her. Her knees threatened to give out. That look could make women swoon. He was leaning against the wall, his arms crossed over his chest. He had short, cropped, baby-fine blond hair, with dark blue eyes. His dark tan told her he mainly stayed outdoors.

"Aren't you hungry, Brooke?" He reminded her of a mythical, Greek god.

"Yes, I am, but I want some answers first."

"Come and sit down. With food in your belly, your mind will focus better."

She couldn't argue with that. She followed him to the kitchen. A long set of windows banked the far wall and highlighted the massive mountains in the foreground. What she saw out the windows was breathtaking. Mountains, some taller than she could see to the tops, others smaller in size, but all of them full of trees, green and lush, was a sight to see. And, she was sure, full of life.

The kitchen itself was impressive with all the latest appliances and gleaming granite countertops. It had a huge island with stools on one side, the six burner gas cooktop on the opposite side. Before her, a feast was laid out. She hopped onto one of the stools and helped herself to a strawberry. Just before she put it in her mouth she challenged, "Aren't you going to join me?"

He laughed. "No. I was so hungry and you were peacefully sleeping, so I helped myself earlier. It's not poison, Brooke. If that had been my intention, you would already be dead."

She shrugged. She had already figured that out for herself and had decided it was safe to eat. She ate her fill and then put her napkin down in her lap smoothing it around in circles. She didn't quite know how to ask it.

"Is there anyone else here?"

"No."

"Who actually took my clothes off? And… washed them?"

"I did Brooke."

She looked up into his eyes. There was heat there.

"Oh," is all she could come up with. She cleared her throat and stood up. She cleaned her plate off. Not knowing what to do next, she returned to the stool.

He said nothing else. His eyes followed her, burned into her skin.

"Um, I suppose I should say thank you. Thank you."

"You're so very welcome, Brooke." He had said the words slow, with heated emphasis.

"How do you know my name? And what is your name by the way? And, where, exactly are we?"

"Slow down Brooke, I will gladly answer all your questions." He looked amused.

She took a deep breath. "Alright then, how do you know my name?"

"I was searching for you. I am a protector."

"Protector of what pray tell?"

"The men who were chasing you, you needed protecting from them didn't you?"

"Well… yes. I guess I did. How did you know I needed protection?"

"I told you already, I am a protector."

This was getting her nowhere fast. He had ruffled her temper. "Listen up, Protector, I want some answers without the runaround, and I want them now."

She had a bad habit of talking before she could fully think about the ramifications. It had plagued her most of her life. She immediately knew she had made a tactical error demanding answers from this man before her. He could break her neck in less than five seconds. Perhaps she should go back to her original brilliant plan. Hide in the bathroom.

He sat motionless and looked at her. "Don't make the mistake of underestimating my sweetness, Brooke. It would bode well not to forget."

She gulped in some air. She slowly got up and backtracked toward the bedroom door. She was getting scared. Hell, she didn't even know his name. For all she knew, he was with the other men, the bad men, all along.

"Brooke, take it easy. I would never hurt you. But I do have my limits and retaliating is my specialty. It would be my pleasure to show you."

He smiled again, dammit. She must have a mild concussion, because she actually had thoughts about what that might imply. She needed to get out of here. She backtracked some more.

He got up. He darted across the room faster than she imagined possible. She was caught in his arms. He forced her to look up into his eyes. His beautiful blue eyes penetrated her carefully built defenses.

"Brooke, listen to me. There's a lot to explain and we have little time before we must leave. I need you to follow my directives for your own safety. All will become clear along the way."

She felt hysterical. She laughed a shaky laugh. He didn't look like he was accustomed to anyone laughing at him.

"Must I prove to you I am in charge here."

She laughed. She didn't mean to, she really didn't. She just couldn't help herself. She must be dreaming. Yes, she told herself. She would wake up any minute now laughing at the ridiculousness of it all.

Then his mouth came crashing down on hers and he took all that she was. He demanded she open her mouth. He pushed his way in, drank like a thirsty man. When she finally softened beneath him, he reluctantly released his hold on her. He gazed into her eyes, and she couldn't have looked away if her life had depended on it.

"Brooke we need to leave soon. Can you please trust me? We will talk further tonight. I promise to make things clear."

He hadn't released her fully. She was still in his embrace.

"What is your name?"

"My name is Dragone."

"Okay, Dragone."

"Okay what?"

"Okay, I will wait until this evening to get all my questions answered. All, Dragone." He released her and she hastily retreated to the bedroom.

He had given her privacy these last 30 minutes. She had a lot on her plate. He would try to make her understand.

"My pack is ready Brooke. It's getting late, are you ready to go?"

There was no response. He moved with speed throughout the house. She was gone. The little minx had tricked him. He was furious. She would pay this time.

Chapter 2

Brooke headed in a general northeasterly direction hoping that would get her somewhere where she could get help. The geography of the land was rugged and harsh. Although it looked picturesque from far away, up close there were knee high prickly bushes, ruts and rocks, and animal creatures lurking about.

Brooke loved the outdoors, and had even camped and backpacked a few times, but always with the luxury of a fully stocked cabin nearby.

The loud silence of the outdoors surrounded her. She could hear multiple crickets chortling, birds chirping here and there, and something that sounded like maybe a coyote howling somewhere far, far away. Stopping near a lake, a moose startled her by taking its massive head out of the water to peer at her. He had underwater grasses stuck to his massive antlers. Sensing she wasn't a threat, he resumed drinking his fill.

Moving on, the trees became denser and the going got harder. Now surrounded by trees and more trees, Brooke was becoming somewhat disoriented. Usually she had her GPS to help guide her. Roughing it was rougher than she imagined. It looked easy enough on the Discovery Channel. Men and women battling the elements, in a quick half hour show that generally ended with the animal saved and the heroes fed.

Maybe the better plan would have been to let this Dragone tell her what was going on. Dragone, who had a name like Dragone? She must be truly scared because she never made fun of other people. Not their names, not their looks.

Brooke was one of those people that always stepped in to defend another's feelings. She demanded equal rights in all matters and for everyone. Men like Booker T. Washington and Frederick Douglas had inspired her. Elizabeth Cady Stanton along with Susan B. Anthony and others had helped shape her life. Patrick Henry, Thomas Jefferson, and Alexis De Tocqueville had impressed in her memorable stories from the past to live by. There were so many people that had helped shape the world in which she lived in. Living with a nice, sane, dysfunctional group of citizens that loved their freedoms is where she laid down her hat and put up her feet.

Pictures of the Women's Suffrage Movement adorned her walls at home, to remind her of the trials and tribulations women had gone through to get the vote.

Once, she had chastised a worker at the Gas and Go station several years ago for not taking the time out to vote in her busy day. Brooke had told her that she wouldn't have a job period if it wasn't for all the good work of her sisters before her. The cashier had looked at Brooke like she had lost her mind. Brooke thought that perhaps the lady didn't have one.

She stumbled, and had to catch herself before she fell face first to the ground. Darn it, she needed to focus and stop her wandering thoughts. They weren't going to get her out of this mess. She needed to think about a strategy. Dragone would be coming, and he would be mad. Really, mad. She had no illusions that he would just let her go. He had this crazy idea, he was a protector. What kind of madness had she fallen into?

After several strenuous miles, she sat down on a fallen log. Sweat was moistening her clothes and she wanted to take another shower, but probably not today the way it was looking. No closer to civilization that she could tell. A town could be just over the next rise, or just a quarter of a mile to the west—which, of course, she was not headed toward.

"What am I doing?" she asked herself. As if to answer, a chipmunk appeared moving through the leaves. "Hello, little guy." The startled chipmunk ran for his life and disappeared.

Dusk would not be far away, she needed to find some sort of shelter for the night. It would be cold once the sun set.

Up ahead there was a winding stream. Not wanting to cross, because she didn't know if she could dry out before dark, she instead walked parallel to the stream until she located a little outcropping of boulders that had vines growing over it.

She would have never spotted it had it not been for the deer that crossed her path near the opening. One buck leading four does to the other side of the stream. Thankful, she quickly looked it over. Wide enough and deep enough, she thought. With no flashlight or matches, she would be at the mercy of the dark until morning, but at least she would have three walls to hide her.

She opened her pack. Opening her little stash of water, she drank sparingly. She had found an almost empty bottle of hydrogen peroxide in the bathroom. She had cleaned it out thoroughly and filled it with clean tap water. It wasn't much, but it was better than nothing.

She had desperately wanted to grab a couple of the breakfast muffins. Reasoning that it would be too suspicious looking if she walked back into the kitchen to get a few muffins, she had let that idea go. Breakfast would have to tide her over until the next meal, that's all. Not too tough. Tough would come tonight, in the dark. She dreaded the thought.

She knew animals and other predators used scent to search for their prey. She put her hands in the stream, brought them up to the surface holding a big clump of clay. Packing it around her fingers, she let the rest fall back into the stream. It dried fairly fast.

Quickly now, for she knew dusk was approaching, she gathered some twigs and broken branches and tried to make a makeshift front to her little fort, to further hide and protect her. She wanted to leave a small opening from the side that she would squeeze into. Her first attempt was a colossal failure. The sticks kept falling down.

After several bouts of trial and error, she found a workable solution. Knowing it needed to continue to look natural, she stacked the branches to hope-fully make it look like it had simply fallen from above. Back pedaling while looking her handy-work over, she gasped. It looked like some totally dumb ass person had gathered sticks and stacked them—totally obvious.

Looking up, "aha," she said. Spotting several boulders on top of the overhang, she had another bright idea. She practically ran up to the top and pushed several off and over. They landed with loud thuds. Scrambling down on all fours she took a branch with dried leaves and spread the tracks she had made coming down the side. Indeed, when she was finished placing the boulders in the front and completely reworking the sticks, it didn't look too shabby.

Needing some water, she sat down and had a small sip. She needed to ration out the water because of all the unknowns. The water might have to last several days if she didn't find a way out of this god-forsaken land. The wilderness needed to stay wild, with her on the outside looking in. With that thought, she took another small sip of water.

Feeling refreshed, she walked as far away from the makeshift shelter as she dared. Walking a short distance into the interior, she spotted the moss she had come for. Using a stick to scrape away some of the moss, she laid the moss off to the side and covered the bare earth with fallen leaves.

After applying some near the top of the shelter so it would appear to be draping over the overhang, she stepped back to survey her job. Seeing several areas that didn't appear to be quite right she again, through trial and error and when she just no longer cared, finished the job and stepped back. She was satisfied it was the best she could accomplish without further tools and know how.

Now done with the main structure, she moved on. She threw the remaining branches in and around the perimeter of the stones to appear as natural as possible. In addition, not wanting to put her fingers on too much, she had used one sturdy branch to move all the other branches, as painstaking as it had been, to minimize her possible scent.

Having some time to kill before dark she decided to watch the stream flow by. Not wanting to venture far, she moved only a little ways downstream. Staring at the flowing water swiftly move downstream, the little ripples that formed as the water would hit a particular rock, was calming, soothing.

If you looked carefully you could see a pattern, depending on the strength and amount of water moving, you would know which rock the water was about to hit. It made her think that all of life depended on the other. *We are all family and we need to take care of each other Brooke.* Where that monumental thought had come from she didn't know, but out here you could easily understand the fragile life cycle and how one thing impacted another.

At home, she thought mainly about how and where to buy her next antique and if the local market would have her favorite fresh fruit in stock next Saturday. Rarely, if ever, did she wonder about the direct impact her and others like her, had on the ever diminishing wildlife. Deciding she needed to re-read some of the books about Teddy Roosevelt when she got home, she looked out over the forest.

Standing still several minutes, she slowly became aware animals came to drink at dusk. At first, she saw a few deer that were a little further upstream from where she stood. They approached the stream with caution, drank with their ears tuned to the slightest sound of movement. They were beautiful, and graceful. She had never witnessed such fragile beauty. It almost made her forget she was lost in the wilderness without any form of communication with the world.

Ten minutes later, she saw two cubs lumbering over to have a drink. They appeared to be young, most likely not alone in the forest. Where was the mother bear? Brooke decided it was past time to go back to the small shelter. The smaller animals were cute; it was the larger animals she was worried about.

Finding several large sticks she used the pocket knife she had found in the bedroom to sharpen the ends and put them in the little shelter, just in case she would find a need for them later.

Chapter 3

Dark was now approaching.

Apprehension started to take over Brooke's good judgment. Maybe she should just find another shelter real quick, like, perhaps there were spiders back in the back. Large spiders, the kind that ate humans lost in the woods. She should have walked on, found a shallow crossing.

Probably a town was just over the next rise, where most people were inside, enjoying good food and friends, right about now. Here she stood, in the dark, cold, stick-filled shelter, with God knows what crawling about where she couldn't see.

She tried to reign in her wandering thoughts, to think about things less scary. But try as hard as she could, her mind kept coming back to thoughts that filled her with anxiety.

Anything could crawl in while she would just be standing there. Things could crawl *on* her here. She wouldn't be able to run out screaming here, alone, in the dark. Reminding herself that there were plenty of big predators she truly had to worry about, and one of them called himself, Dragone. That thought woke her up to reality, like a bucket of cold water thrown in her face.

Calming down, she decided to think about things logically. She needed to decipher this puzzle. Who were the men that had attempted to nab her? Maybe, they had wanted to kill her.

There was one certainty in all this mess; Dragone could have killed her at any time. It didn't make much sense that he intended to hurt her. But, she had run from him anyway. He scared her. Oh, he had scared her down to her toes. A shiver ran down her spine just thinking of the reaction her treacherous body had displayed. Never feeling so strongly a reaction to a man before, she was totally out of her element here. All he had done was smile at her that first time, and her mind had sent all her nerve endings screaming for more.

The dark was becoming all consuming. As hard as she might, she could no longer see more than a foot or so in front of her. Now, her hearing had taken the forefront and she could hear loud sounds she didn't like. Scurrying, shuffling, little sounds, that at night sounded ear piercing. Jeez, why didn't she stay in that house; why didn't she just give the guy a chance to explain? But, she knew why. Because he had kissed her; and she had liked it.

Growing up, her life had been filled with love. No doubt about it. Her most treasured family consisted of two cousins and an aunt, who, together, formed a happy tightknit family. Her aunt tried to fill all the emptiness she sometimes felt not having a mother and father like most of her friends.

Her cousin, Jacqueline, was an interior designer, and a great one at that. Although she didn't live near her, they talked every chance they got. Jacqueline had plans to visit her this summer. They were both amateur history buffs. They had plans to visit several antebellum homes in the surrounding area this coming summer.

Her cousin, Claire, lived in the northwest. She worked as a paralegal, with long hours, and sometimes she even brought work home. She wished Claire didn't have a job that was so demanding. It had been at least three months since the last time they had spoken. First order of business when she got out of this nightmare would be to call her; hopefully, go see her soon. She missed Claire.

And then there was her aunt. Aunt Sissy was the sweetest woman on the planet as far as she was concerned. Unfortunately, she had been dealt a terrible burden to carry in her later years. She had early stages of dementia, which required a live-in caregiver. She checked in frequently with the caregiver and always spoke to Aunt Sissy several times a month. It had been six weeks since the last visit. She needed to get over to Aunt Sissy's house soon. Aunt Sissy would be worried about her, maybe.

Brooke was one busy lady these days after all, she reminded herself. She owned her own antique store and was very proud of the fact. Struggling eight years to save enough money for the startup fund had been hard enough, but then formulating a safe business plan was downright frightful. If she could survive all that, she should be able to survive just about anything, she reminded herself.

Ashley was minding the store while she was gone, thank God. Ashley was a great girl. About eight months ago, Ashley had walked in and inquired about the "Help Wanted" sign she had hung outside the store window. She was midway through college, seeking a degree in Business—trustworthy to a tee.

Helping with both inventory and stock left Brooke free to find more treasures. She combed the countryside looking for unique pieces to compliment her store. She had a steady list of clientele that demanded her constant attention to detail. Mrs.

Morton was waiting for Brooke to find her just the right piece for her foyer. Brooke had her eye out for a 42" round wooden table with claw feet and inlay design. The list went on and on. She desperately needed to get back to her shop.

Ashley was probably frantic by now, no doubt. She needed her cell phone. It was an experience she never wanted to go through again. How did people back fifty years ago survive without a cellular for god's sake? She'd had a cell phone by her side since third grade. It was mind boggling, just down right inconceivable to be without a cell phone.

She heard something—something scary, something getting closer. She decided it wouldn't hurt to say a quick prayer.

Chapter 4

Dragone wasted another ten minutes gathering food supplies. He was still furious. He would not accord her anymore privacy. He didn't have time for this nonsense. His first order of business was to secure the safety of Brooke.

Getting her to safety was paramount to her delicate feelings. Not understanding the inner workings of the female mind, he had distanced himself from an early age. He knew it would be useless to try to grasp, as he had a logical, practical mind, where everything was black and white. The best he could figure, women's minds were in every color of the spectrum.

It shouldn't take too long to reacquire the little minx. Still fuming, he came to the first rise, when he felt the first stirrings of trouble. Like an expert, he calmly became one with the land. Seemingly melting into the landscape he laid down flat, motionless. He turned his head very slowly, scanning the perimeter in small increments for the vermin.

The Ones were seemingly in endless supply. The rebellion was, indeed, making headway to curtail and even suspend some of their activities, but much still needed to be done. The groundwork had been laid, the organization was growing, and soon he hoped they would finally gain the upper hand.

The Ones were beings of another species that walked amongst us. They hid themselves and their agenda in plain sight. The Ones had politicians in all three parties and had people in positions of power throughout the government and within law enforcement as well.

The Ones hid themselves well and were a well-oiled operation. They methodically moved in circles to instigate and aggravate the masses. They manipulated lawyers, doctors, even veterans, to their cause. They pitted politicians against one another. They thrived in being the catalysts of global skirmishes. They were in essence, all that was wholly evil. Their strategy was simple and brilliant. No one was the wiser. Their reach was far and wide.

Movement. He saw what he was searching for. The abominations were now cautiously coming toward his locale. Three of them; he was going to enjoy this.

Moving slowly, with the strength of his forearms, he scooted to a more defendable position. He slowly, quietly, removed his diamond-powered device. It had been dubbed, the "KO," by his fellow soldiers. It was compact and lethal. The device had been created as part of a collaboration of the great minds of both Trevor's and Victoria's forces. Victoria, Brooke's cousin, along with her husband, Trevor, had combined their forces in an effort to defeat the Ones.

Victoria had provided some of the specifications for the KO. They had recently acquired a new cache of diamonds from the Forgotten Caves that had a very unique set of properties. The device, the size of a small cellular, would send a charge into its victim, dissipating the water content such that the bones were compressed. The rest he wasn't sure of; he just cared it killed the Ones. Unfortunately, it did have limitations; it drew a lot of energy. The Ones could detect its usage once fired. And the length of time it could be fired was limited as well. He was hopeful these features would be enhanced soon.

They had top notch men and women working around the clock researching and building new devices. Several teams worked together in various areas of expertise such as weaponry, research, IT, military, political strategies, security, etc. to make the organization stronger.

Through a small opening between the rocks, he could now see them approaching. About fifty yards out the one on the left signaled for them to come to a halt. Splitting up, they were approaching from three sides now.

He waited patiently. The moment the first one moved out of the line of sight from the other two, he struck hard and fast. The device effectively eliminated that one.

Virtually soundless, he disappeared from the face of the earth, just like that. There was a shift in power in the atmosphere that could not be helped. Knowing that the others would immediately know something had taken place; he gave up his position and stood up, to the surprise of the remaining Ones. Quickly, efficiently, he blasted both Ones almost simultaneously, and wiped them off the land.

Feeling quite satisfied, he replaced his weapon and proceeded onward. The device was fresh out of the research lab and still needed major tweaking, but there had been a greater need to get the device into the waiting hands of the rebellion.

Walking onward, he found her trail. It shouldn't take very long now.

Chapter 5

Her heart was pounding so loud it was deafening. She forced herself to silently breathe in and out. Whatever was getting closer was taking his sweet time about it. Some large animal was rummaging through the forest. Now she could hear small grunting noises. What if it was a bear, or a bobcat? Did bobcats even make grunting noises? She wished she had paid more attention to the Discovery Channel. She felt for the sharpened sticks behind her and slowly and quietly moved one closer to her and put her hand around it. She readied herself. The animal was definitely getting close to the opening now.

Throughout the years she had experienced a few times where she recognized she had an affinity for animals. An idea came to mind. Maybe she could somehow mentally push the animal in the other direction. She was desperate enough to try anything.

Like a river rushing to the ocean, she felt a change in her thoughts. One minute she was thinking she should mentally push the animal away, and the next she felt a stirring in her mind and a change in the atmosphere around her. She was mentally pushing the animal away somehow. It was totally insane.

Now determined, she focused on that power and directed the animal to seek another direction. The creature made a grunting noise, as though he didn't like being nudged in the opposite direction, but nonetheless, turned reluctantly back toward the direction it had come, and moved off far away into the woods.

She forgot to breathe. Gulping in several deep breaths just to focus, she became euphoric. Wanting to dance in the moonlight, sing to the stars, shout to the forest, she could talk to the animals just like Dr. Doolittle. Well, not actually talk, but she had communicated with an animal, sort of. It was amazing. She would go on the Late Night talk shows and people everywhere would request interviews. She would be famous.

"Hellooo" she said out loud. Even if it were true, not that she actually knew for sure it was really true, but even if it were true, she would never tell anyone. She would never be left alone. And, someone, somewhere, would want to test her. Yuck, no way. Silliness aside, she probably imagined the whole event. Being this scared, in the middle of nowhere, without a cellular, without a match or flashlight, would cause any reasonably sane person to hallucinate.

Just as she was gathering her inward strength, she heard another noise. Not anything like the former one. This noise sounded distinctly manmade, perhaps a four-wheeler. The noise was growing, building in strength as it got closer. Maybe it was Dragone looking for her. Somehow, she wasn't comforted by that thought at all. But no, this felt like evil. The hair on the back of her neck and arms rose. If she left her hiding place, the person would easily find her. He had lights, she didn't. Breaking her leg trying to outrun a four-wheeler probably wasn't the brightest idea. No, she would stay put.

She could see the lights now, off in the distance, but increasingly closer to her makeshift hideout. It was one of the men who had tried to kill her; she was sure of it now. Shaking uncontrollably, she tried to melt into the back of the small shelter. Forgetting all about the spiders, she tried to push herself up against the far wall that was just some jutting rock formations. Whatever, ignoring the pain, she saw and heard the four-wheeler approaching. If Dragone appeared right now, out of the blue, to again save her, she might even kiss him, she thought.

The four-wheeler stopped downstream. With the lights facing the stream, a large man stepped out of the four-wheeler and began to walk around looking at the ground. He seemed to be analyzing something. He spoke into a device, "Hey Austin, this is Mike, her prints end here. She's probably nearby. Should I try to engage her, or wait for you? Okay, roger that."

He walked back to his four-wheeler and sat down. After what seemed like an eternity, he turned it on, crossed the stream, and slowly moved on.

Brooke could no longer see the four-wheeler. Where did he go? How the hell had he followed her prints? In a four-wheeler, in the dark, he had followed her prints? Didn't he mean tracks? But how could anyone follow tracks in the dark, in a machine no less? She thought trackers walked on foot, looking at the tracks. Or, a tracker could use dogs to track with their keen sense of smell. That man had done neither. None of this made any sense whatsoever.

Unsure what to do next, she closed her eyes and just listened. Forcing her to calm down, the sounds of the night rushed in. There, in the distance, was a slight noise that was out of place—a mere whisper on the wind, but distinct nonetheless to her ears.

It was someone approaching from above. She was sure of it, but unsure what to do. With her stick in hand, she readied herself. Funny though, she didn't feel the same as when the man in the four-wheeler had come near.

Adrenaline pumping through her veins like rushing water, she steadied her shaking hands.

The person was making a beeline for the structure now and was just about on top of her. The air around her was filled with some kind of electrical charge and it was surrounding her. Maybe that's why she hesitated, just long enough so the stick didn't pierce his heart. She forced herself to hold back the stick as she realized it was Dragone. He jerked the stick away and threw it down on the ground.

Whispering he said, "What are you trying to do, kill me?"

Ignoring his tone of voice and so relived Dragone had come for her; she practically threw herself on him, hugging him. She cried with joy and relief that he had come. He had come.

Surprised, he awkwardly embraced her, and returned the hug. He lightly patted her back like he was unsure what to do. He whispered in her ear she was safe now; it would be okay. They stood there for only seconds, but Brooke felt a shift in her heart. He was getting to her and she didn't even like him all that much.

Maybe that was why he hadn't given her a scathing lecture yet, not that he had said much else, she thought as they crossed the stream. How far did voices carry through the night anyway? She wondered silently why he would cross the stream when the man in the four-wheeler had crossed but decided not to open her mouth. He had taken her hand and directed them in a different direction than she had originally been taking. She could barely keep up, let alone speak.

After they had crossed the stream, he had quietly told her the Ones were doubling back to the location of her hideout and they needed to get as far away as possible. He told her not to speak for any reason. Just to follow him without question, if she wanted to see another sunset.

She quietly pondered who the Ones he had spoken of were. What could they possibly want from her? She was just an antique shop owner for god's sake. How did he find her? How could he see to walk? She couldn't see anything. Blindly, she stumbled beside him, hoping not to fall and take him with her.

Did these Ones perhaps want some priceless antique treasure she stumbled upon at her shop? That didn't make any sense. Surely, they already would have retrieved it from her shop. If that was the right scenario then why would they be chasing her all over the countryside? But… maybe the priceless treasure came in a pair, and she was needed to locate the second item from a cankerous dealer that only she could deal with.

She needed to stop thinking too much. She didn't think that she was very good at international, high level, spy stuff. Probably these guys mistook her for an identical twin. Maybe they were looking for an identical twin that fought the world over, working for various governments to rid the world of crime lords, or maybe evil dictators that had come to power. It was said that there was an identical twin out there somewhere for each person. After all, there were billions of people on earth.

They seemed to walk all night, but in reality it was most likely only a couple of hours. Her feet were so sore; her muscles were screaming so, pleading for a rest. Dragone had his back to her since crossing the stream. Having not spoken a word, but keeping a tight hold of her hand, the silence was becoming annoying. She couldn't stand it any longer.

She yanked lightly on his grip. He completely ignored her. So she yanked much harder the second time. Stopping, he turned to look at her. After a few seconds of assessing her, he turned and resumed his pace. Being pulled along for about another twenty or thirty yards, it took all her energy to stop him.

This time he leaned in to her and whispered, "What is it Brooke? Bad guys behind us you know."

"I need to rest. I can't possibly keep this pace up. I can't, Dragone."

He looked her over thoroughly this time. He turned his head and looked out over the land, thinking.

"Alright, Brooke, I know you're exhausted. Can you keep up for just a little while longer, until we reach the base of the mountain chain? There, I can find us shelter. They can find us too easily if we stay here, out in the open."

"Yes, I think I can make it. Thank you for coming for me. Thank you." She said it quietly, a mere whisper in his ears, but he heard.

He regarded her a few seconds more and then said, "You're welcome Brooke, but that doesn't mean I won't exact payment from you. You will pay for the trouble you have put me through this day. Mark my words, Brooke."

A slight shiver ran down her spine. She wasn't sure if she should really be scared or not. Somehow, she didn't think so. Her best defensive move she generally applied when someone made her nervous was to challenge the person. Before she could think of a smart-ass comment, he pulled her forward, and once again resumed his maddening pace across the landscape. Along the way she focused on great comeback lines and was somewhat disappointed she didn't care enough to say anything once they stopped.

Much later, to her poor feet's delight, he stopped by a fallen tree. Gesturing for her to sit, she didn't argue. She hadn't felt such happiness at being able to sit down ever in her life. Who would have thought the mere act of sitting could bring such joy? He surveyed the land and walked back over to her.

"Can I trust you to stay put while I take a good look around?"

"Look it's your fault I left in the first place, buddy. I can take care of myself... until you get back." She had put as much smart-ass emphasis into it as she could muster.

He nodded his head and walked off. He was gone from her line of vision almost immediately. She was a pain in the butt. If she were him, she wouldn't even bother to come back. He could be watching a football game right about now with some pizza and beer if it weren't for her. She sure hoped he wasn't tired of her yet. "Please, please, come back," she whispered.

Time went by slowly. She couldn't figure out exactly how much time had expired, but she knew it had been a very long time. Too long for Dragone to have just taken a brief look around. Something was wrong.

What should she do? Continue to wait or try to find him? The sky began to slowly change colors. From the dark pitch of night, she could just make out shadows across the land. Then, she could eventually see a blue streak in the sky, as if the sun was trying to erupt.

Standing up and stretching her sore muscles, she looked around in all directions. Having no idea if she should stay or leave, she sat back down for another half hour or so.

There was no way Dragone would not come back for her. Something or someone was preventing him from doing so, she just knew it somehow. But what would Dragone do? What would he want her to do?

Daylight was brightening to the point most things were visible. The shadows were now taking shape. She was in fact near the base of the mountains, but definitely exposed where she currently sat. The Ones would be able to spot her from very far away. Whoever the Ones were.

Chapter 6

Moving with a sense of urgency, she climbed up what seemed like Mount Everest, but in reality it was probably roughly only 25 to 30 feet or so. Painstakingly she climbed, because she felt she would be able to see more of the terrain. The top didn't originally look very far up, but now that she had started her trek up to the top it seemed to be miles away.

She inched her way one rock at a time. At first, she was able to scramble up on all fours, but it soon became apparent that she needed to slow down and actually use toe holds because the terrain was becoming too vertical for her to maintain her balance.

A rock from above came rushing down straight from directly above her. Trying to move out of its path she lost her footing and slid several feet down. Grabbing at anything to stop her momentum she was able to hold on to a prickly bush that dug into her hands.

Stopping abruptly, stunned and shaking, slowly she looked around. Not more than six inches away from her position was a drop off that most assuredly would have plunged her feet first to her death. Or perhaps worse, she would have fallen breaking several bones and would have been alive but unable to walk away. *Thinking that way would not be good,* she reminded herself.

"Focus, Brooke," she quietly said out loud.

Brooke realized she would not be able to simply start a decline down, but would, in fact, be forced to either continue her slow procession upward or she could attempt to go parallel until she found a way down. Brooke looked at all her options and decided she would try for a ledge that was about another 12 feet or so above and slightly to her right. Please, please let the ledge hold a small cave, somewhere to hide, to rest. She slowly, and painfully, putting one small handhold and toehold at a time, was able to gain purchase.

Maybe, she could locate some sign of civilization from up there. As she approached the ledge she was afraid to put her hands on the ledge. What if the ledge was loosely imbedded in the side of the mountain and it came crashing down on her. There was certainly no place to go but down if the ledge was unstable.

The view down was horrifying. Looking down had been a huge mistake. *Don't think about it. Don't think about, Brooke.* But now that she had looked, she couldn't put it out of her mind.

She imagined the ledge would give way and she would be propelled down the mountain-side along with boulders and rock debris that would cut her and dig into her body as she screamed. The descent would be painfully slow and she would feel every cut, every abrasion.

She would see her end as she descended to the seemingly bottomless pit where animals were awaiting her arrival. They would devour her as she lay there helpless. "No they are *not* waiting for you Brooke. Shut up and get a grip," she said out loud to no one in particular.

"I must order new supplies next week. Ashley has finals coming up and I won't have her help." Brooke tried to think about normal things. Not, that she was alone on a damn mountainside trying to get away from the Ones. Surely she must be in some Twilight Zone or maybe she was in her own private Ground Hog Day episode. Or worse, maybe she was in the Matrix and they hadn't told her yet.

The more she tried not to think too much, the more ideas popped into her head. She decided she was going to get a full massage experience as soon as she got home.

She tested first one side using her right hand and then with her left hand. It seemed sturdy enough, but was it enough to take the full force of her weight? Not knowing the best course of action, she took a leap of faith and propelled herself up and over the ledge. It held. Nothing shifted. No tiny pieces of rock went raining down.

She scooted back away from the edge and looked around. There was a small oval shaped opening behind her. Only large enough to crawl in and the light only showed a very brief look into the interior. It looked less and less appealing. Halfway expecting a cougar or bear to come out any second now, she thought about finding a new, newer hiding place.

Pain laced her brain, finally finding the time to let her know her hands were bleeding and thorns were embedded in three fingers. Two of the thorns were shallow enough for her to squeeze and push the thorns close to the surface. She was able to remove them with her finger nails.

However, the third one was too deep and she pushed the pain aside. Later, when she was sitting in a cozy chair, reading an intriguing, good book, having already showered and ate, she would take it out.

Looking out from her position she could see quite a distance away. Nothing was moving around down there that she could see. Quiet. She had never been anywhere, this isolated from people, with only the rugged beauty to see.

Her extent of the great outdoors in previous encounters had consisted mainly of girl scout outings and hiking about 3 miles to a waterfall once on a vacation in Hawaii. She had had a tour guide along with about twenty other people with her, on her one huge excursion into the wilds of Hawaii.

This was so much different. Never having faced a situation with no help to call for, she felt off kilter. She needed her cell phone, dammit. Even if her cell didn't work here, she still would feel more secure just knowing when she arrived somewhere, anywhere near civilization, she would once again enjoy all the rights and privileges said cellular provided.

Indeed, the view here was nothing short of breathtaking. Even with the level of fear she felt escalating, she appreciated the beauty; it was impossible not to.

She spotted movement and discovered she was watching her very first coyote running through the underbrush. He was magnificent. He had a somewhat elongated muzzle, scruffy brown fur, with cute ears. He seemed to be running at full speed.

Looking intently in front of the coyote, she tried to locate what he was chasing. Seeing nothing moving she looked elsewhere. What she saw when she expanded her viewing area, were several men jogging behind the coyote several yards back. They had their eyes on the ground, like beagles hunting for fox.

Falling flat on the surface of the ledge, she peered down carefully. They were running right for the location she had spent the night. Once they reached the area, they spent several minutes walking around the spot, studying it. This was bad—really, really bad.

She could do nothing but watch from above. If she tried to move higher up they would be able to spot her easily. Panic was setting in big time. The men turned their heads in all directions, taking it all in. Conferring with each other they moved in unison toward her direction.

Oh no. What should she do? She looked around desperately and all she saw was the dreaded cave entrance.

"Go, there, go there, Brooke." It was a whisper she barely heard. Her eyes were wide as she looked first this way and then that way. No one was with her here on the ledge. *I did hear something, Brooke. I know I did.*

Nonetheless, she crawled inch by inch as flat to the ground as possible, over to the entrance. She took a deep, steadying breath, staying low to the ground and forced herself to crawl into the pitch black hole.

The interior at first was wide enough to accommodate her size. It was hard trying to crawl through because the rock formations were tiny protrusions that dug into the heels of her hands and dug into her knees each time she landed on one.

All of a sudden, the opening became considerably smaller, to where she had to squeeze and suck in her gut, just to push her way through. Not to mention the thoughts racing through her mind here in the total darkness about bears and mountain lions. "Stop it Brooke, no bears or mountain lions can get in here. What is it with all these animals anyway?" she softly spoke out loud, as though speaking out loud reaffirmed it was true. Talking to herself was a testament to her willpower to try, try, try, to keep it together. But..., what about bats? They would love a nice cozy cave like this wouldn't they? Those vampire bats, did they kill people? Or would they just leave her alone, if she left them alone?

Without any warning she tumbled two or three feet down. She had a moment of sheer terror that left her breathless. She quickly realized she was fine. She couldn't see anything but she could breathe easier. Guessing that either it was a larger interior room of some kind, or there was another exit bringing in outside air.

She didn't really care. She scooted over until she felt a wall and put her back up against it. She hugged her knees and rested her head; she was mentally and physically exhausted and numb. How much longer could she take this level of stress? She imagined what the war-torn countries of faraway must experience on a daily, weekly, yearly basis. How did they cope?

Drifting off to sleep for a few minutes, she awoke with a start. Scared senseless now, she counted to twenty just to bring her heart rate down. Hearing nothing and seeing nothing was paralyzing her. Stiff arms and legs wouldn't work. She gently rubbed and forced her legs and arms to work again. Not knowing how long she had actually sat there frozen, she thought about crawling back through the opening to find out what those monsters were up to.

She felt fear somehow, creeping into every space of her being. It engulfed her like a bad smell. Her imagination started to get to her. She envisioned the Ones doing chilling, horrific, things to her—things that only death could save her from. Her hands started to shake. This time she was out of luck. Dragone was nowhere around to save her ass this time.

Feeling around there wasn't so much as a good-sized rock for her protection. Being far too scared to venture farther into the cave, for there were too many possible disasters waiting, she instead opted to wait for whatever would happen. She was just so weary, she knew she should be doing something, anything—but she just couldn't rally to the challenge.

Chapter 7

She heard a slight shuffling sound. It became louder and louder until she heard a god awful shriek. It was mind-numbing and painful. She instinctively covered her ears, but it did no good. It was horrendous. Not human. It was like some animal that she had never heard before; then, absolute silence. Afraid to move an inch, she waited. Hardly breathing, because she was sure someone or something would hear. It was then she heard a tapping noise—no wait, not tapping, hammering. They were going to widen the space enough to crawl in.

No longer caring if she made any noise, she got up on all fours and gingerly moved forward, desperate to find a way out. Her hands only met more space in front of her. It was tedious and slow. And the hammering was becoming more pronounced, faster paced. They could hear her moving about and knew they had her.

She would fight until they killed her. She would not leave this place with them. She couldn't. She wouldn't. No matter what, she needed to find a way out, now. She kept at it, but there was nothing and nowhere to go. She sat down exhausted and defeated. They were coming and she couldn't stop them.

Then she felt it; a slight breeze on her arm. That could only mean that there was another exit. *Please, please don't let this be a cruel joke*, she pleaded. Resuming her four legged stance, she moved forward with determination. Feeling her way carefully, the mostly dirt floor became rockier. Little pebbles bit into her hands and knees. As she moved forward she began to see something. Up ahead, a tiny pin prick of light beckoned.

She kept her eyes trained on that beautiful beam of light. She imagined it was calling to her. As she came closer, the beam of light began to change shape. It was growing and widening. It was a most glorious sight. At the end of the cave she found herself shielding her eyes, until she could focus on just the light that came through her fingers. Slowly, she unraveled her fingers and was able to look out into the daylight.

She was on the backside of the mountain and still very far from the ground. Looking up, she determined it was safer that way even if it looked to be somewhat vertically sheer.

Anything was better than finding out what those guys would do to her once they caught up to her. Remembering her pack was on the ground back in the cave in the dark, she decided time was running out. She must move forward, and fast.

She put one foot out and grabbed a small rock crevice and held on for dear life. The men were getting close to squeezing through. She felt the urgency moving through her mind. After climbing a short distance, she began to sweat. Sweating was not good for her hands. Rubbing her hands on her shirt each time she grabbed another hold was slowing her down even more.

Not far now to the top. She could just make it out when she heard a loud triumphant yell. They had made it through. Rushing now, she practically leaped to the top and heaved her body over. It was grassy.

Wasting no time, Brooke jumped to her feet and took off running. Trees, tall pines were everywhere. Caring not for the consequences of running all out, she put as much steam into her run as possible.

She was going downhill now, forced to slow her pace somewhat for fear of running into one of the hundreds of trees as she went flying past. They would be right behind her. They had looked fast when she saw them jogging behind the coyote.

Bursting through the trees she stopped abruptly when she saw a trail marker. That meant she was close to civilization. She followed the trail marker disregarding her instinct to run straight ahead. When it became apparent the trail wound through the forest at a leisurely pace, at how she assumed hikers would enjoy spending their day, she gave up her new direction and opted for the running straight down the mountain strategy as fast as humanly possible. She couldn't hear her pursuers but was too afraid to stop and look back for fear of what she might see.

Chapter 8

Dragone had gone approximately three or four miles when he felt the Ones close by. It was a familiar, sickening push in the air around him. One he wished he would never have to feel again.

Moving off the path and finding a place to hide, he waited to take stock of the situation. He didn't need to wait long. The Ones were in a group of about a dozen men and they had plenty of fire-power. Someone in the organization wanted Brooke acquired quite badly to go to all this trouble.

He pressed his back up against the boulder as they approached from the north. He slowly pulled the safety latch off the KO, his eyes never leaving his prey. If he had to, he would take out as many of the Ones as possible before they got to him.

They moved off, going right past him, with no indication that they had seen him. He wasn't fooled. He positioned himself facing the other direction and waited. Two Ones came at him all at once. They shot him square in the chest and he felt a pain that was indescribable. Pushing that pain to the farthest reaches of his mind, he eliminated both Ones quickly. More would follow. Thanking the gods above, for his Kevlar vest, he knew the bruising would be a bitch in the days to come.

Two more replaced the former two, and another came up behind him. Managing to eliminate just one more, was three down, nine to go. He realized those weren't the best of odds, right before he was knocked out from behind.

He woke to the Ones kicking and punching him. He took a strong kick to his kidneys and couldn't breathe for a second or two. Determined to go down fighting, he surged to his feet and twisted the head of an Ones, which fell where he stood. They intensified their efforts and made him pay for killing one of their own.

He was surprised to wake up alive. He came awake in increments, like his brain was trying to compartmentalize his different pains into sections so he couldn't feel it all at once. He lay motionless on the ground and tried to take stock of his surroundings. Two men sat at a table with a four-wheeler parked in front of them.

Even if he could get to the men undetected, he strongly doubted that he had the strength to overtake both men before one of them could take him out. He lay there gathering his strength, beginning to formulate a plan of action; then, he felt her presence.

No doubt in his mind, she was here. Of all the stupid, ignorant, dumb ass things, she had disobeyed him once again. Why couldn't she listen? Had he not distinctly told her to stay put? Now, he would be forced to yet again revise his plans. Dammit, no wonder he had stayed away from females for the most part all these years.

Chapter 9

After what seemed like many miles, she had to stop just to breathe. She heaved in and out. No way could she keep up this pace. Her legs were threatening to give out at any moment now. Her legs felt rubbery like a rubber band. Her mind was having a hard time focusing. She needed food and water. Where were those men? Why hadn't they overpowered her yet?

She forced herself to move forward, for there really wasn't any choice. The hair on her arms and neck told her danger was close. Way too close. Stopping mid-stride, she hunched down and cautiously looked around. No sound was emitted but she knew, somehow, that Dragone was near. And, he was in trouble.

Not wanting to examine exactly how she had come to know this information, she filed it away for later inspection. Right now, she had to figure out how to help Dragone.

Moving forward very cautiously, she saw small, tiny, whisks of smoke. As she approached, she saw an embankment. Below the tree line there was a small encampment. A small camp fire was nearby. Not far away, lying in the dirt was Dragone motionless. He looked like a Mack truck had hit him. His eyes were swollen, so much so, she doubted if he could see out of them. Various cuts and scrapes with blood oozing out of them marked his body; she wanted to rush to his side.

She had this overwhelming urge to see how injured he was; to give relief any way she could. Instead, she forced herself to focus on the rest of the encampment. There was a four-wheeler parked nearby with two men sitting at a nearby table and chairs. They didn't seem to be alert to anyone approaching.

She sat back on her heels and assessed the situation. She knew from the look of things no way would she be able to overpower those two men. They looked strong and mean.

Dragone really looked to be in bad shape. He wasn't even moving. Maybe he was unconscious. If he was, then what would she do? Even if she was lucky enough to get to him, if he was unconscious, it would do no good. Picking him up, let alone carrying him, was impossible, even on a good day.

She peered back down into the camp. The men still seemed occupied with whatever they were looking at. It appeared to be some kind of weapon. They were turning it over repeatedly, trying to make it work. She looked over at Dragone and knew instantly that it was his weapon they were intently trying to figure out.

Maybe, she thought, that might just be enough of a distraction to get to Dragone. She needed something, in way of a weapon though. Over by the four-wheeler she spotted a knife sitting on top of the roof near the rear of the vehicle. She gauged the distance to the four-wheeler to be about 25 yards. She could slip over to it and pick it up undetected. She just needed to be really, really quiet.

As if walking over a bed of coals, she felt every step, along with the need to hurry. It was burning her feet. It would cause her to stumble, fall to the ground making a loud thud. The ground became her whole focus because it wanted her to falter. Each individual pebble, each protrusion coming up from the earth, along with the little dimples, the small tiny crevices in the landscape that would turn your ankle; they were forces all working against her, wanting her to fail.

Walking that invisible tight rope that was threatening her balance, she cautiously approached the four-wheeler. Not wanting to take too long for fear they would stop being preoccupied, she moved over and ever so slowly removed the knife. She had it. The momentary elation was instantly replaced with fear as her brain refocused on the Ones.

She hunched beside the four-wheeler and decided to move behind some rocks and try to come up behind Dragone, so as to hide as much of herself as possible. It was a long and tedious journey. Small branches, fallen leaves, and uneven terrain all worked against her. She had to focus on every movement. Her whole life came down to those steps to Dragone. Nothing else mattered.

Sweat formed tiny beads of perspiration overtop her brows and it caused her to have to wipe her eyes with her shirt to better see. The trek was tedious and so scary. She couldn't believe she was actually crawling over to this man, about to save him, maybe. Maybe was a big if. She knew the men would probably pounce on her any second now, and she would be at a loss to do anything.

Brooke moved inch by inch until she was almost upon him, when he snaked out his hand, and firmly touched her arm. Letting her know he was awake and fully aware she was there. She should have known the guy was awake. Nothing seemed to faze him. Not even what appeared to be the beating of his life.

She put the knife into his hand. He felt for the hilt of the knife and took it from her. Positioning his hand back to his front he froze when one of the men stirred, repositioning in the chair. Brooke didn't dare breathe, praying he didn't look their way. He didn't.

Brooke moved back and away until she could hide behind the boulder. Thinking she could best help Dragone if she moved closer to the men, she worked her way back over to the four-wheeler. Each movement brought a moment of fear. Fear that the men would turn their way, or hear her clumsy attempt to hurry.

To her surprise, on the front of the four-wheeler was a weapon of some type she had never seen before. It was lying carelessly on top of the hood. It looked sort like a mini flashlight but it had a handhold that was skinny in the middle and fat on the two ends that flared out at the tips. It had a rough texture and glowed slightly in the middle when she picked it up. It was definitely some type of weapon, not a toy.

She came to the end of the four-wheeler and waited. There was no time to try to figure out how the weapon may work. Having faith, she just hoped she would be able to make it work if she needed to. If not, she would make use of her bare hands as best she could. She could not and would not leave

Dragone to fight alone in his time of need.

Dragone heaved his body up and lunged for the men. It was amazing, considering he looked like death warmed over. He moved like a lethal animal fixed on his prey. He was able to overpower the first one, killing him instantly, but the second one moved back. It gave him enough time to pull out a weapon and point it at Dragone's head.

Brooked screamed. Without hesitation she pointed the object at the aggressor. A beam of light flowed out from the tip and exploded into the man. He fell hard against the ground, limp.

The kick threw her backwards at least 2 or 3 feet. The result was that her head collided with a sizable tree. She had to shake her head just to focus. Stunned it had worked, she just stared at the man. She had never hurt anyone ever before. It didn't feel good.

Dragone seemed to be stunned too, as he gazed over at Brooke. She was an amazing woman. And, she had just saved his carcass.

He went to the fallen man and determined he was dead. He gathered his weapons from the table, then grabbed his pack and threw them up and into the four-wheeler.

"Let's go. Now Brooke!" he screamed to get her attention. She was just staring at the two dead bodies. "The Ones are fast approaching. We only have seconds now."

Brooke hopped into the four-wheeler, pushing away what she knew she had just done to that man. She would dwell on this newest blight on her soul later—*much later*.

Quickly fastening her seat belt, Dragone was already speeding across the terrain. She was bouncing around so violently her teeth were chattering. She didn't understand the hurry. She needed to look Dragone over, apply some ointment and bandages. Maybe a butterfly stitch or two would need her attention. Almost craving to eat and drink, as she hadn't eaten since breakfast the day before, she was beginning to feel light headed from lack of food, or more likely, perhaps from the non-cooperative tree.

Thinking she would fish around in his pack, hoping to find something to munch on, she reached back and saw what the hurry was all about. The men were pursuing them in their own four-wheelers. They were coming hard and fast. She forgot all about her hunger and screamed to Dragone.

"What can I do to help?"

He looked briefly over at her. "Get the Maxon—and point it at them."

"Get the what?"

"Get the Maxon—and point it at them. It sort of looks like a flashlight." The Maxon was the weapon she had picked up from the hood of the four-wheeler.

Dragone refrained from mentioning it was the same weapon she had just killed the Ones with. He imagined it was her first kill, and there would be hell to pay once her mind had a chance to refocus.

Brooke undid her seat belt and immediately was knocked up against the dashboard. She had to hold onto the seat head rest with one hand as she grabbed the so called Maxon, Dragone wanted her to shoot.

She pointed it toward the advancing four-wheelers. Once again, a beam of light flowed from the tip and small explosions lit up the rugged path. One four-wheeler was forced into a tree and the second four-wheeler veered just in time to avoid hitting the four-wheeler head-on but couldn't stop in time to avoid hitting the tall oak tree next to it.

Staring back at the two four-wheelers, she continued to shoot the Maxon until Dragone forced it from her hands. He gently lowered the Maxon, putting it on the backseat, and gestured for Brooke to sit down. She buckled up and looked forward not saying a word.

He would not think about the female beside him. He knew she was hurting. Hurting badly. Killing had left a bad taste in his mouth as well in the beginning. Now, he was just a killing machine with no emotion. Emotion was for the weak. Emotion got you killed. And staying alive was one of this man's main goals in life.

Brooke said not a word. She was in her own little world with dead men all around. Their souls cried out for justice, for her blood in payment. She had done the unthinkable. She was now one of the monsters. How could she go on living with herself? What would her cousins and aunt think of her? They would be crushed by the revelation that she had actually killed another person.

She could never live with this burden. Maybe she should tell Dragone to take her to the nearest police station. *I need to be locked up like the murderess I am.* Oh god, had she really killed that man? This couldn't be happening.

She should be back at her antique store right now, not here. She didn't belong here. Why her? What had she ever done to deserve this? Someone had her confused with someone else. Someone bad perhaps—someone not like her.

She loved and gave generously. She would never harm another intentionally—never. But the reality of it, that she had in fact, done exactly that, was starting to rip her insides apart. The tears started to flow silently down her cheeks. Letting them flow, she imagined they would wash her sins away.

Dragone was relieved Brooke had finally fallen asleep. She had been crying for some time now. He didn't know what to say to her—how to comfort her. It had stirred feelings in him he hadn't known he was capable of. He actually wanted to pull over and comfort her somehow. He hadn't. He needed to get her to safety; her feelings were not important. Not his priority. When he delivered Brooke, someone at headquarters would deal with her. He would be free of her soon and would be happily fighting and killing the Ones once again. Killing the Ones was safe; he knew how to deal with monsters. Dealing with women was a much scarier proposition.

He continued to drive another hour until he came to a dirt road. He turned left at the fork and parked behind the tree a few miles on down the road. Brooke didn't stir, even when he turned off the four-wheeler and called her name. Lines of exhaustion were plain on her face.

He needed for her to wake up because he was worried about possible dehydration. He roughly unbuckled her seat belt and called her name. Nothing. Cursing himself, that he should have taken better care of her, he picked her up in his arms. He remembered she was as light as a stick of butter in his arms. Looking down at her sleeping form, he knew tonight would be rough on her.

He walked up the steps of the house and gave a verbal command. The door opened into a room rich in furnishings and textures. The main part of the living space had vaulted ceilings that soared twenty feet up. Several couches positioned around the see-thru fireplace with Persian rugs scattered about. The kitchen was a high-tech marvel.

He moved to the hallway and picked the first bedroom he came to. He laid her on top of the comforter and placed one half of it over her. He didn't think she would appreciate waking up to being undressed twice. Besides, he owed her a thing or two.

He pulled up a view of the outside perimeter on the laptop and scanned it carefully. Satisfied, he took a much needed shower and dressed in jeans and a tee. In the kitchen, he pulled some staples out, made himself a sandwich. He sat down in the living room and helped himself to a glass of scotch.

Why had she put herself in harm's way to help him? What did she expect in return? It made no sense to him. No possible way had she actually just wanted to help. Not one person for as long as he could remember had ever saved him before. It was foreign to him, uncomfortable even. He did the saving. He sat there a long time thinking things over.

She awoke to a beautiful bedroom. Sitting up gingerly, she looked around and down. She still had her clothes on. The room itself was about fourteen by eighteen feet. Tastefully appointed drapes and matching bedding. She spotted an au suite bathroom and helped herself.

She needed to take these clothes off and burn them or at least wash them before she could possibly wear them again. Looking around she spotted a dresser on the far wall. She found some tees that went down to her knees and not anything else she could wear.

She took a shower and towel dried off before putting on the blue tee shirt. She padded down the hallway and peered into the main living area. She saw him then, sitting in a chair, holding a glass of liquor. A bottle in front of him and it was a quarter empty already.

"Come join me, Brooke. You probably need a drink, too."

"Yes, I do actually. But first I need to wash my clothes, if possible."

"Sure, help yourself. The washer is in the laundry room next to the kitchen. All the supplies you'll need are there already."

"Thank you."

He couldn't reply. He now saw her walking in his tee shirt across the floor toward the laundry room. The tee hiked up as she walked and he imagined she would wash all her clothes which meant she had nothing on underneath that tee.

She felt self-conscious as she emerged from the laundry room upon seeing his roaming eyes looking only at her legs. She darted behind the kitchen island and asked if he had a bathrobe she could borrow.

He looked at her several seconds before he responded. "What did you want again, Brooke?"

"I asked if you have a robe I can borrow until my clothes are done."

"Oh. No, sorry, but I don't own a robe."

He doesn't look sorry. Very happy, in fact, she thought. She would have to walk around like that at least an hour or so while she waited on her clothes.

"Say, is there anything good to eat, I'm starving."

"Help yourself. I had a peanut-butter sandwich. I think there's some jelly in the pantry over there." He pointed to a small door behind her.

"Oh. Thanks, I think I could eat two sandwiches, I'm so hungry." She ended up fixing only one sandwich and got a bottle of water. She moved over to a stool on the far end of the island so not to allow too much of a view for Dragone. She didn't want to invite trouble when he was clearly drinking plenty of the scotch.

"You don't have to be afraid. I told you before, I would never hurt you."

"I also remember you referencing something about retaliation."

"Yes, I did, didn't I?" He didn't elaborate further. He was looking intently into her eyes.

"Yes." She looked down at her sandwich until not a crumb was left. When she looked back over his way, his eyes were still on hers. She had this funny feeling down deep inside. She practically jumped down from the stool and hurried over to the laundry room to put her clothes in the dryer. Thankfully they would be done soon and she could get dressed. Being in nothing but his tee shirt was putting her at a distinct disadvantage. She couldn't even come up with a few good smart-ass remarks.

"I think I'll just wait in my room until my clothes are done, if that's okay with you." She moved in the direction of the back rooms.

"No. It's not okay with me. Come. Come here and join me." He patted the seat. When she didn't move, he added, "please."

She came to the couch farthest from him and sat down. She pulled her knees up and pulled the tee shirt over her legs at the same time. This way most of her body was now covered and she could bury her head behind her knees.

"I have some questions for you."

"I have some questions of my own," replied Brooke.

"I will answer your questions, Brooke."

"Good. Start by telling me just who you are, really. Don't give me the protector crap. Tell me what's really going on here."

"Do you really want to know the truth, Brooke? Are you sure you can handle it?" asked Dragone.

No, she wasn't sure about anything. Everything in her world had turned upside down and she didn't know who to trust, who to turn to. She couldn't grasp it all. Not to mention the part where she had killed a man. Her eyes started to water just thinking about it.

"Yes, I want to know."

"Alright, then. You already know my name. I am a protector; I have been assigned to you. I am to bring you back with me to a more secure location where you can speak with your cousin, Victoria."

"See, I knew it. I just knew it." She pumped up and down in her seat she was so relieved. She continued to pump until she realized the tee was seriously riding up. "You have the wrong girl. This is all one big mistake." She was so elated. *All—one—big—misunderstanding.*

She would go home tomorrow and forget the whole horrifying ordeal. Go back to her antique store and sell her interesting antiques and live her interesting, quiet life. Never to be bothered again by crazed men with high-tech weapons. No more running for her life. No more Dr. Doolittling. Just back to being Brooke, plain ole' Brooke, the nice girl who owns the antique shop down the block.

"Oh, I'm sorry. I meant to say Claire. Her real name is Victoria, however. That's what we all call her."

"Huh." Her mouth fell open. She stared at him. *Did he just say, Claire? Her cousin, Claire?* She must have heard him wrong. "Did you just say, Claire?"

"Yes, Brooke. I said Claire. Your cousin, Claire. There's also a cousin named, Jacqueline, I believe. You also have an Aunt Sissy as well, don't you?"

Her head was spinning, she felt lightheaded. This couldn't be happening. There had to be some mistake. Maybe she was just dreaming a nightmare and would wake up at any moment and laugh about believing it was real. She'd get up and go to work just like she did most days of the week. Have a cup of coffee down the street and speak with her fellow shop owners about the days' events.

"Brooke. Brooke! Look at me."

She reluctantly looked his way, her daydreams whisked away. This was not a dream. She was in the middle of a real-life nightmare.

"I know this is a lot to take in at one time, but time is what we have very little of. Do you want to lie down for a while before I fill you in further?"

She rallied her defenses. "Go ahead, let me hear the rest."

He seemed undecided but continued on. "The Ones, as I mentioned before, are hunting for you. I was sent to bring you in safe and sound. The Ones are beings not of this world, and they need you and your cousins to further their evil ways."

Now, she knew he was crazy. She had just started to believe him. Oh. My. God. She was in this house with a mentally disturbed individual, wearing almost nothing, no less. He was probably a stalker who had zeroed in on her family for some reason or maybe no reason at all. Crazy people did crazy things after all, didn't they? And even though he didn't look crazy or talk crazy, what did she know about it. Maybe all crazy people were smooth talkers and good-looking in their own way.

He saw the look in her eyes. "Listen, I am not a lunatic. It was hard at first for your cousin, Victoria."

"Sure. I just bet it was. Look, I think I've changed my mind. I do need to lie down, if you don't mind. I'll be back in a little while." She started to rise.

The look he gave her genuinely scared her. He was pissed. "I do care. Sit down now, Brooke." She started to speak. "And, shut up too. I don't take too kindly to someone questioning my integrity."

He tried to soften his look when he recognized fear rolling off Brooke in waves. "Listen, I know it sounds crazy but hear me out. Don't make assumptions based on just a few statements so far."

For the remainder of the time, she sat still and paid attention.

"For the record, I too, had a hard time believing in the Ones before I met a bunch and found out the hard way. I'll tell you my story. A few years back, I had just gotten out of the service and was visiting a buddy of mine. He lived on a house boat in San Francisco. He wanted me to help him pick up some supplies he found for sale on the internet. When we arrived at the address, something didn't sit right with me. I told him to leave, forget the damn supplies. He told me I was nuts. But I knew. I knew something was wrong there. He got out of the car before I could convince him otherwise. Long story short, he died, I survived."

"The Ones didn't mean to kill him I don't believe. They needed him. You see, he was a nuclear physicist. I have hated the Ones every day of my life since. Of course, the problem was, I didn't know they were the Ones back then. I just thought a bunch of strung out junkies had attacked us. And, that's the problem most people have. The Ones hide themselves well."

"Haven't you ever wondered about all the increased violence taking place in our world? I used to think it was just tied to the population growth. Now I know the truth. Your cousin will fill you in. It's hard to take it all in right now, but trust me, it's the sad truth."

She didn't know what to say. He certainly seemed to believe his story. She wasn't convinced.

"They need your cousin, Victoria, because she is the granddaughter of a set of twins that were born with Ones blood. She is a chosen one. You, Brooke, are special as well. You have powers you don't know about yet. You are not a chosen one, but you can be used to breed more Ones, as you too, have some Ones blood running through you. Only a select few can be used for such purposes. Your family's special makeup made your real biological mother a prime target. Your mother was killed when it was determined she would not be healthy enough for their purposes. However, they wanted you."

"Someone from the rebellion saved you and gave you a home you could be safe in to grow up. Your family's secrets have come to light and all of you are at risk. Hence, that's where I come in. I stand ready to serve and protect." With that he saluted himself, and took another swig of his scotch.

In time, he continued on. "Victoria is strong. She helps lead our people against the Ones. She continues to amaze us all. Someone has been dispatched to bring in Jacqueline as well as yourself, so don't be alarmed for her. In addition, before I left, I was told Aunt Sissy was in route to our headquarters, as a precautionary measure."

He was a little bit tipsy. He sat up and started to pour some more Scotch into his glass.

"Don't you think you've had enough Scotch for one night?"

"Probably, tonight is a Scotch kind of night for me." He stopped mid-stride and put the bottle down. "You do this to me. It's your damn fault, you know."

"Just, what, exactly, is *my damn fault*?"

"The Scotch. I need it to distract me from you. I never drink on the job."

"Are you kidding me? Your excuse for getting tipsy, is me? Well, Dragone, I'd say it was your own damn fault."

With that she got up and hurried over to the laundry room and her clothes. She firmly closed the door and got dressed. When she emerged, feeling more confident now, she told Dragone that she really sincerely thanked him for all his help thus far but she needed to get back to planet earth where work was waiting for her.

"Look Dragone, I know you believe that story you've just spun, and maybe it is true. I don't know. But what I do know is that I need to get back to my shop if I want it to continue to make a profit. I rely on that income and I don't have time to run around being chased by these Ones, as you call them. To me, they just look like thugs. "

"They probably mistook me for someone else. Maybe they're drug dealers and they think I have valuable info to some missing stash; or maybe some henchmen are trying to get to me because I accidentally witnessed an assassination unknowingly. See, I can come up with some hyperboles too. It's not that hard."

He just sat there quietly contemplating how to make her understand. He knew it seemed unbelievable. "When I last spoke with Victoria, before I embarked on this mission, she warned me you would be skeptical. She had a key phrase she told me to repeat to prove to you I had spoken with her. She told me of a story your aunt used to tell you. She played pretend with you and your cousins and told you, 'to call for your uncle Larry' should you ever feel scared."

"Your aunt, who knew what dangers surrounded all of you, made you memorize a phrase you each learned from an early age as code for help: '*I need to call my Uncle Larry,*' your cousins, your aunt, and you had in case of an emergency."

Brooke froze. No one knew that. No one but the four family members themselves knew that code phrase for an emergency.

She whispered softly, "how do you know that?"

"I told you, Victoria told me. I know it's confusing, but your cousin told me so you would come willingly with me. We must not delay any longer. Tomorrow morning we will need to leave at first light. Can I trust you Brooke, not to try to run out on me again?"

She couldn't answer truthfully because she just didn't know.

"I didn't think so. You're in my bedroom you know and that's where you'll stay tonight, next to me. If I have any problems, I will not hesitate to tie you down. Are we clear about that?"

Instead of seeing fear in her eyes as he had wanted, she seemed really, royally, pissed. She was fuming with outrage.

"How dare you. You are the most infuriating, insufferable, arrogant man I ever have had the misfortune to run into. Who do you think you are? No one ties *me* down. Do you hear me, you arrogant oaf. You're a behemoth pig-headed jerk. I will cut off your balls and feed it to the coyotes if you dare to touch me. Are we clear about *that*?"

For the first time ever, his mouth hung open in a sort of state of shock. He couldn't believe what he was hearing. This little spit-fire with the beautiful chestnut colored hair, shapely hips and rear end, and those ever so soft looking legs, was threatening him—a killing machine that few people dared to cross.

He would have had murder in his eyes if anyone else had said that to him. He wasn't sure what a behemoth was, but by the way she had said it, it must be insulting.

She threatened to cut off his balls. She had called him a behemoth, pig-headed jerk, and an arrogant oaf. He looked at her and started to laugh. He didn't intend to laugh, he never laughed, not since childhood. It started out small, like his vocal chords were practicing. Not just a chuckle or a light-hearted laugh. No, this was a full throttle laugh that came from somewhere deep inside, and burst forth from him to fill the room with outrageous laughter.

Tears started to form in the corner of his eyes. He choked a couple of times and coughed, and then had to wipe the edge of his eyes again. It felt freeing to chuckle. She made him feel wonderful. It was Brooke that changed him in many small ways, chipping away at his rock hard façade.

He didn't know when he had ever been so moved to laugh out loud, let alone such a deep throated laugh he did not recognize as coming from his own mouth. Man, she was something else. This woman was certainly unique in his eyes. He absorbed her essence with each inhale of breath, and wanted more.

Her look told him she didn't appreciate him laughing at her. He laughed harder. It took him a few minutes to force himself to calm down. His stomach was starting to hurt. The whole scenario was so damn funny.

"I'm so glad I have provided amusement for you." She glared at him with her hands on her hips. "Don't ever speak to me like that? I am normally a friendly, easy going gal. But *no one* tries to bully me. I won't stand for it. I know I owe you for saving my life, but I draw the line at rude and crude."

"Okay, okay. I give up. I'm sorry. I was just trying to scare you anyway. I wouldn't tie you down—unless, you asked me to, of course."

He smiled. He had dimples. Those cute little dimples reminded her of her first boyfriend from the tenth grade. She had replied, yes, when he stunned her at the lunch table one day, and had actually asked her out. It had been a disaster date.

"Trust me, I'm not asking."

She moved toward the bedroom and closed the door, firmly. He waited ten minutes before he got up and went to the bedroom. He fully expected the door to be locked and was surprised when it wasn't. He entered and found Brooke lying on the far side of the bed. She looked fast asleep, but as he sat on the bed, he saw her stiffen in response. She couldn't fool him.

He took his time taking off first his boots and then his pants. He stretched out in the bed. Brooke was lying as still as the dead, fully clothed. He tried to remain on his side but he was a big man used to lying toward the middle of the bed. He finally gave up trying to stay on the edge of the bed. He wouldn't get any sleep this way. He slowly gravitated toward the middle and felt Brooke's immediate response.

First, she stiffened more like a tree trunk than an itty bitty slip of a woman. Second, she tried in vain to roll to the far edge. She kept slowly rolling back until she finally gave up and they both settled down.

Brooke could feel his feet touching her, his hairy legs rubbing up against hers. It was awkward to say the least. His weight was pushing her toward the middle of the bed. His arm and hand were lightly touching hers. She tried in vain to analyze her reaction to him. Somehow it comforted her and she soon fell fast asleep.

He waited until he heard the slight change in Brooke's breathing that told him she was finally asleep. He fell into a light sleep himself as he knew with confidence he would wake if Brooke tried to get up. He was trained to wake at the slightest noise. She could not escape him this time.

In the middle of the night he awoke to a sort of keening sound. He looked to Brooke with concern. She was still asleep. She started to cry out in pain.

He shifted his body and brought her close. He held her. Shaking her slightly, he continued to tell her she was just dreaming, to wake up.

"Brooke, wake up honey. You're having a bad dream, that's all."

She woke up wide-eyed, breathing way too fast. She looked into his eyes.

"I was surrounded by dead men. All of them wanted my blood for my sins. I killed one man I know of, possibly two. I'm going to hell. I'm a bad person. You should take me to the police station right now. I deserve to be put away. What happened to me? I was always a nice person before I met you."

"Shhh, it's alright Brooke. Everything is going to be okay." Holding her, he thought, *I have every-thing under control.* He simply had to hold her and soon she would go back to sleep. He could do this. He held her and was ready to go back to sleep when she started to cry. *No, no, no,* he thought. *Not crying. I can't take a female crying.*

"Please Brooke. It's okay. Don't cry. You're not a bad person. That man was going to kill me. You saved me. If you hadn't shot him, I would be a goner, and you, Brooke, would be in a breeding program."

That made her cry—even harder. *Good going, dumb ass,* he thought.

"Listen Brooke, you're safe and those men will never harm you again. I won't let anything else happen to you." He sure as hell would try to keep his word.

She seemed to settle down a bit, so he continued. "I will just hold you, so you'll know you're safe. Now come here, a little closer." He moved a little closer as did she.

"I will hold you like this." He moved his hands over her head and held her protectively.

"See no one would dare bother you tonight with such a bad-ass here."

She sniffed and settled in some more. He waited until he heard the steady rhythm of her breathing that told him she was asleep at last and then he slowly drifted off as well. His last thought was that he had never had a woman in his bed this long before. And, never one that was fully clothed.

Chapter 10

Brooke woke to a comfortable spot in the bed that felt warm and heavenly. Realizing Dragone was holding her, panic set in momentarily; her body tensed in response, until she remembered how tender and reassuring he had been during the night. Relaxing into the mold of his arms she sighed.

The dream had led her to the riverbank where the dead souls of men rose out of the water. They seemed not to be able to leave their watery grave, but they screamed and demanded she be punished for her sins.

She couldn't remember quite all of it, as her dream had already started to fade, but she did remember a name—Jonathon. But for some reason her memory couldn't quite grasp it and the rest eluded her, like a tree branch that you aimed for as a child, but it was just a pinch taller than you could reach. One thought was stuck in her mind though: Jonathon; somehow she knew he had wanted her to remember his name.

Dragone had held her lovingly. *Why did that word, lovingly, pop in my head?* No, he had wanted her to stop disturbing his sleep and he had been looking for a quick fix. That had to be it. He didn't seem to be the gentle type. Yet he had gone to the effort of comforting her, instead of demanding she quiet down.

He was certainly a complex man, capable of extremes, to say the least. She could hear his light snoring. She had never spent the night with another man, nor heard a man snoring. Liking the soothing sound, she snuggled closer to Dragone and felt at peace. She audibly sighed. Something she had never experienced before in the arms of another.

He knew she was awake when she moved closer and made a cute little sigh. Dammit he liked her. She felt right, lying here beside him. She fit. These feelings were so foreign to him. He didn't understand how she could be affecting him so. He needed to stay focused. Stop letting this little minx get under his skin. And he needed to get her the hell to headquarters as fast as he could.

A half hour later he got up with some regret. He had already stayed there longer than he should, but had been unable to resist. He headed for a cold shower when Brooke spoke from the bed.

"Dragone, I know I have been a lot of trouble thus far. I am having a most difficult time assimilating all the components of your story. But I know, after telling me what Claire or Victoria told you, that at least you have, in fact, spoken with my cousin. I have, therefore, decided to follow you until I see her for myself. I… I want to thank you sincerely for saving me time and again."

He moved over to the bed and sat down as she hurriedly scooted over. "You're welcome. And, I want to thank you, as well. No one in all of my sorry-ass life ever saved me from anything."

By the look in his eyes, she knew he was telling the truth. "You're so welcome. How about you take your shower and I will make our breakfast?"

"It's a deal."

An hour later, having eaten and showered, Brooke felt back to normal; whatever that was. Normal had always in the past meant that her store opened and closed on time. Her expenses were held in check and her profits at least paid all her bills. Normal was waking in the morning alone with the radio and keeping her own hours. Normal was seeing the same people every day with the same basic pattern every day. Normal was the four seasons that never deviated much in her part of the world.

Dragone called from down the hall, "Can you be ready to leave within thirty minutes, Brooke?"

"I'll be as ready as ready can be," shouted Brooke.

"Good."

They were back to barely speaking. Both feeling uncomfortable with their new found friendship, Brooke tried to stay busy. She cleaned the kitchen until it was the former perfect condition she'd seen when they had first arrived. Straightening up the laundry room and the bedroom as well, she thought Dragone should at least contribute by cleaning up the living room, seeing how he had messed it up with his scotch bottle and glass the night before.

Dragone cleaned up the living room when he realized she would not pick up his scotch bottle or wash out his glass. *I can't blame her for being perturbed; my sorry ass was a little tipsy. It was irresponsible of me dammit.*

She had little to pack so she was ready in less than twenty minutes, sitting quietly by the front door when Dragone came from the bedroom. He had an extra pack in his hand.

"Here, this will work much better than carrying a plastic bag around. I found this in the closet. He handed the pack to Brooke. I hope it's alright. A little small but that way you won't be carrying too much weight around on your back."

"Thanks. It's just fine."

"Sure, no problem."

They weren't even looking at each other now. Last night it had felt wonderful when he had held her while she had cried. But now, this morning, she wasn't sure what she felt. It was that uncertainty. How did he feel about it? Did she just annoy him or did he care a little? Was she making too much out of nothing? Or, was this the beginning of something?

She had never gotten this far into a relationship with anyone else before. She was treading new territory here. Her life up until now had been filled with accomplishing her life's goal of owning and operating her own antique store. Dragone was probably sorry for his actions last night and couldn't wait to get her delivered to wherever they were going. She needed to stop making something out of nothing. This was a job to him, plain and simple; she needed to remember that.

He filled his pack with food provisions, gathered his weapons, and indicated he was ready.

"We will head west for the rest of the day. We'll stop at a place I know. We'll spend the night at a vacant safe house on the outskirts of Sangnesta, a small town not too far from here. We can't stay in mainstream, because the Ones have their tentacles spread out far and wide. They would almost instantly know our location."

"Oh. Well, okay then. I guess if all the safe houses are as nice as the last two, I really can't complain."

"Sure you could, but it's nice that you won't."

They left then, heading west. Using a jeep from the garage, it was more comfortable than the four-wheeler had been. Thinking about the four-wheeler reminded her about killing, so she immediately thought about nothing for a while.

It was mid-morning when Dragone asked her if she would like to stop at the coffee shop. Needing to use the Ladies room, she enthusiastically agreed. He stopped at a fairly busy gas-n-go store to minimize the possibility of being recognized.

Before they got out he handed her a broad-rimed hat that was too large for her head. Just happy to get out of the jeep and stretch, she did not complain. They were only there about eight minutes before they headed back out onto the road.

At two o'clock Dragone pulled off the main road and parked in a vacant lot. He pulled his pack forward and started handing Brooke some food stuff. She prepared two sandwiches which consisted of gourmet peanut butter and jelly. There were two ginger ales and some water. She preferred water over soda any day of the week. She drank the water; he had both ginger ales. Neither seemed in the mood to talk; so, having eaten their fill, they resumed their travel.

An hour went by until Brooke tried to start a conversation. "Dragone, tell me a little bit about yourself. You seem to know quite a bit about me already."

There was no indication he had heard her. No movement of his head or otherwise. He didn't respond for several minutes. She bit her tongue. *Why did I even ask him? He's an ass! I'm not going to speak to him again! Not for any reason!* Imagining more colorful words with which to describe him, to her surprise, he started to speak.

"Brooke, I'm a very private man. Normally, I don't tell anyone about my past, but I will answer your questions. What would you like to know?"

Recovering from her shock she said, "Well, you can start with your childhood. Where's your family? How many brothers and sisters do you have?"

He hesitated just enough that she took note of it. "I lived with my grandparents until I graduated from high school in Indiana. Shortly after gradua-tion they were killed in a car crash. When the estate was settled and all the bills were paid, there wasn't much left. My cousins took me in until I enlisted with the Marines. I've been back a few times but I no longer think of it as home.

"I'm so sorry. Do you have any siblings?"

Again, there was a slight hesitation. "No." *At least, not that I know of.*

"Well, I have two cousins, but no siblings. I used to wish for a dozen brothers and sisters. Although my cousins are like sisters to me, we all understood our mothers and fathers were missing. We did the best we could under the circumstances but I always felt lonely on Mother's Day and Father's Day celebrations at school," added Brooke.

She looked over at Dragone, then down. All those polite manners her Aunt had instilled in her seemed to have flown away somehow. Brooke seemed to need to tell Dragone more and more about herself. Why, she didn't know. Very few, in fact, knew anything about her family or her past.

"I'm so sorry I interrupted, please continue."

He glanced over at her and smiled. "That's okay, I like hearing about your family. Victoria has told us some stories but I'm sure there's still a lot I don't know about. By the way, she told me to take very good care of you, or else."

Brooke smiled at that. "Yes, Claire, I mean, Victoria, this is so confusing by the way, is very protective of her family. She was always our appointed protector."

"Once, at school, a bully made fun of me because I didn't have a mother. I knew better than to let it get to me, but this particular bully had a strategy that I wasn't prepared for. He told me his father knew my mother. He even told me her name. He said my mother had been his father's bitch. I ran all the way home and cried myself to sleep. I refused to tell anyone why."

"The next day, Claire skipped school and went to my school at lunchtime. She walked right up to Robert and punched him in the gut. When he got up off the ground, she kicked him in the knee cap. Then, she leaned over him, and told him to bring roses to my house and apologize. He was to tell everyone at school he had lied—needless to say, he never bothered me again."

"Wow. She's something else. I see it runs in the family." He looked over at Brooke and smiled that smile that said much more than she was willing to consider right then. She blushed at the thought.

"So…tell me about how you came into this line of work, Dragone."

"After my stint in the service, I found a job at Emcore Industries. It's a little firm in Santa Monica. My boss was friends with one of the team members of the rebellion."

"After about three months John finally approached me one day and asked me to join him for lunch. Little did I know, I had already been thoroughly investigated and approved for submission. Initially, I had a hard time believing the whole story just like you, but eventually I saw the light. I found out later that they had been watching my whereabouts on and off since my grandparents death. The Ones had had a hand in my grandparent's death."

"How?"

"The Ones had staged the crash to acquire a scientist. Only he wasn't a scientist quite yet. See, they wanted this sixteen year old kid that was brilliant. The parents stood in their way, so they devised a plan to remove them. My grandparents were just the innocent victims that were at the wrong place at the wrong time."

"I'm so sorry. Did they get the sixteen year old boy?"

"Yes."

"That's awful." She didn't know what else to say. The whole scenario was sad.

"My abilities came in to play around twenty-one. I…"

"Whoa—wait a minute. What abilities?"

"I have some abilities that you may think strange. Some would call them psychic abilities. Some would call it something else."

"Wow. That's amazing."

"What no, 'you're crazy' comments? No, 'sure, yeah, right' comments?"

"No, none." *I can't very well tell you you're crazy when I think I'm crazy too.*

"You have abilities as well, don't you?" He looked at her then, really looked at her. Shock was plainly written on her face. *Yep, she has abilities no one knows about.*

"Tell me Brooke."

"I…Well…I mean I don't really know for sure, but I think I might possibly be able to somehow communicate on some elemental level with animals."

"Wow. I'm not sure what I expected you to tell me but that sure wouldn't have come to mind. Brooke, that is a most unusual and precious gift. Tell me about it."

"I am telling you this but I have never told anyone else ever before, not even my family. I guess if you can share, so can I." She hesitated but trudged forward.

"I always seemed to have a special bond with animals from the time I was very little. Animals just seemed to like me. I guess that would be the best way of describing it. Cats and dogs in my neighborhood always greeted me and seemed to pay more attention to me than to their owners when I was around. Anyway, I didn't really think too much about it until I was in the woods alone the other day."

"It was dusk as I hid in that little makeshift hut. Soon after dark, I heard a rather large animal ambling its ways near where I was. I was very frightened at first but then an idea popped into my head. I decided to try to mentally push the animal to change directions. I felt some kind of energy all around me grow and to my utter surprise the animal grunted his displeasure, but nonetheless, turned and went back the way he had come."

When he didn't comment she said, "I know, I know, that's probably the craziest thing you've ever heard, huh?"

"No Brooke, not crazy at all. I myself have that ability."

"What? What are you saying? You can communicate with animals?"

"Yes. Yes, I can Brooke."

Neither spoke for at least an hour.

When Dragone finally spoke Brooke nearly jumped through the roof. "I could teach you a few things. I mean…, you know, to help you along—if you want me to, that is."

"Um, yeah. Yes, I would like that very much actually, Dragone." She didn't know what, if anything, he could really teach her, but she was curious enough to see what he could do. The whole thing sounded so farfetched, but yet if he could really talk with animals…

Brooke was so lost in thought for a while that she almost missed the sign up ahead that said, "Albuquerque, New Mexico, 169 miles." "Hey, is that where we're headed?"

"Yes and no. We will pass Albuquerque and drive on to Sangnesta to the vacant house I told you about."

Chapter 11

They decided to stop at a little mom and pop diner with a gas-n-go attached. After filling the gas tank, Dragone parked facing toward the highway. As they walked toward the door she saw that from the outside looking in it looked like a real Mayberry diner. Inside the diner, there were several booths, with about a dozen stools up against the countertop. It looked like an original 50s diner complete with Formica countertops and chrome appliances.

There were little individual jukeboxes in each booth, with a selection of rock-n-roll music to choose from. The upholstery looked like it had seen better days; otherwise, the place seemed well kept and clean.

"Howdy folks, welcome to Sally's Diner. My name's Betty, what can I get you folks to drink?" She put the rag down she'd been cleaning the countertop with and hid it underneath the counter.

As they took their seats she noticed Betty was an older, slim woman that seemed lost in the 50s. She had a beehive hairdo for god's sake. She had never actually seen a real live beehive hairdo before, except in a book of hairdos throughout history. *Doesn't she know what century it is? We aren't in Mayberry are we?* Brooke thought. She had to admit it was kind of cute on her, but she was willing to bet that hair didn't get washed very often. *That* wasn't a very pleasant thought.

"I'll have some lemonade please," replied Brooke.

"I'll have a coke, thank you," said Dragone.

After ordering, Brooke sat back and relaxed. They had been traveling for forever it seemed and she had been more uptight than she had realized. Looking around, she realized this diner was the real Americana of the Midwest.

It was a typical mom and pop restaurant on the outskirts of anywhere. Probably just eking by, just enough to pay the bills, but probably not enough for a vacation. And so, this was more than likely their whole life day in and day out, never experiencing the rich cultures and life found elsewhere beyond their sleepy little town. Brooke wondered what these people in here would think about other beings walking around trying to get the upper hand, trying to take over the earth.

There was a television on in the corner, by the far set of stools. The stools were the 50s type stools.

You know, the silver and red round stools that kids love to swivel in. The TV channel was broadcasting the news. Brooke hadn't seen the current news in a very long time. She tried to hear what was being said but they were seated too far away so she finally gave up and turned her attention to the décor in the restaurant.

She had been in several small mom and pop diners before. Back when she was a kid, her Aunt Sissy used to take them down to Woolworth's Diner on 5th and Commerce. Aunt Sissy had told her it was a replica of the real Woolworth's Diner from long ago. It had been similar to Sally's Diner in that it had 50s décor with bar stools at the counter and several booths surrounding. It had pretty much the same old black and white checkerboard linoleum flooring, raggedy booth seats, and fixtures with chrome shining everywhere. And a similar old timey cash register where Aunt Sissy's money would disappear and Brooke could never reach.

The food arrived and Brooke noticed Dragone was looking out the window intensely. He spoke without looking away from the window and whatever he was searching for. "Brooke, please fold our food in napkins and carry it. We are leaving, right now." He stood up.

"Ma'am, excuse me ma'am, can we have the check please?" asked Dragone.

The waitress responded with a questioning look but said nothing. She gathered the bill and brought it over.

"Is something wrong with the food? I'm sure Tom cooked everything right nice like."

"No. No, everything is delicious. We just realized we are way behind schedule and we need to get going, that's all," said Brooke. She was stuffing her backpack with soggy fries and greasy hamburgers. The drinks were in disposable cups so she let Dragone grab them after laying money on the table. They hurried toward the jeep and climbed in.

"What's wrong Dragone? Why the rush?"

"The Ones are close by."

"Where? In the diner?" She glanced back at the diner.

"I'm not sure. There was a man sitting in a booth at the far end of the diner but I never got a good look at his face." He put the car in drive and headed out back on the road. He kept glancing in the rear view mirror.

She settled into her seat and took the food out and laid it on the console. "Maybe you're imagining things. I didn't see anyone suspicious."

"No, the Ones were somewhere close by. We need to get as far away from there as fast as we can." He grabbed one of the burgers, removed the napkin, and started wolfing it down. In between a mouthful he said, "Brooke, we can't stop again unless absolutely necessary. Aren't you going to eat?"

"Yes." Brooke took out her hamburger along with some fries and started eating. *How my life has changed in just a matter of a week. I have to contact Ashley and check on my store. I need to let her know I'm safe. That's funny—safe. Am I safe with Dragone? I hope I made the right decision.*

"What are you thinking about? Are you regretting your decision to believe in me?"

"I don't regret my decision Dragone; I am just feeling uncertain of my future I guess. As long as my life didn't take drastic turns, I have always felt in control of my life. Even if a family member passed away and sadness crept in, there was still control. I could always make choices and redirect my life the way I wanted it to go. This week changed everything I imagined I controlled. Now I know, I have next to no control over my life—none. I'm scared Dragone, for the first time in my life—I'm really scared."

Dragone didn't want her to be scared, but her reality was that she should be scared. "Look, I don't want to sound negative or anything, but if the Ones get their hands on you it would be a disaster."

"I know, at least I think I know. But I don't understand it all. How am I a candidate for their so called breeding program? Why me? How could Claire, I mean Victoria, be a "chosen one?" What about Jacqueline? And, Sissy? I just don't understand? This is like a waking nightmare I can't shake off." She put her head in her hands as if the motion would somehow make it all go away. She shook her head and then leaned her head back against the headrest and closed her eyes.

Dragone just drove. He didn't understand women. Why did she need to know? It didn't matter why, it just mattered she get away. He looked over and saw that although she had slanted her head toward the window he could still see a single tear silently rolling down her cheek. *Damn, not crying, I don't like crying. Shit, what do I say?* In the end, he decided not to say anything and just drove.

Brooke finally appeared to be asleep when Dragone saw a speeding car in his rearview mirror. He pushed down on the accelerator and gunned it. Brooke woke up with a start.

"What's wrong Dragone?" She looked out the window.

"We have company coming." He looked in his rearview mirror.

Brooke turned and saw a black SUV weaving through traffic and coming fast. *Oh God, now what?* she thought. She made sure her seatbelt was tight and stared forward.

"Get the Maxon out of my bag in the back, on the floor Brooke." Dragone kept the KO safely under his seat. The KO was too powerful and dangerous to put in the hands of anyone not trained in its use.

"What are you crazy? There are people on this road. If I use that horrible thing people are going to get hurt! Maybe worse," she added, but she had said the last more quietly.

"We just need it ready, just in case we are forced to use it."

She reluctantly took it out of the bag and sat it on her lap. The SUV steered recklessly, weaving sharply in front of cars with barely enough room to do so. Cars were beeping their horns loudly in retaliation.

As the SUV maneuvered into the left hand lane, Dragone went to the right lane. He waited until the SUV was almost side by side until he swerved sharply to the right at the last possible second and took the off ramp to highway number nine. The SUV could not get over fast enough; the terrain was hilly, filled with desert shrubs and jutting boulders scattered throughout the landscape, not suitable for the SUV to try to cross over. It was a delaying tactic at best, but, at least for the moment, they appeared to be safe.

After a short period of time he took an exit and headed toward the downtown area. He stopped at a garage and pulled his jeep right into the bay area. An elderly gentleman walked up to the window.

"Hello, my name's Earl. How can I help you folks today?"

Dragone got out of the car and told Brooke to stay seated. He walked with Earl toward his office area, his arm around his new found friend. Brooke couldn't hear what was being said. Dragone walked back a short time later and told Brooke he had sold the jeep in exchange for another car Earl currently had available. He had made it worth Earl's time.

Brooke gathered all their belongings and moved toward a minivan that had stickers all over the back window. Obviously, a family had previously owned it. It had silhouettes of a mom and dad along with two kids and a dog on the far left side of the rear window. There was also Ron Jon and South of the Border stickers and several Disney stickers as well. Within minutes they were back on the road again.

"We will take the back roads now. We don't have too much farther to go. I'm sorry but we can't stop again. It's just too risky."

"That's okay. I can wait."

Chapter 12

Victoria, Brooke's cousin and the chosen one, approached the Ones with renewed determination. She had come to this place of worship to protect the innocent among them. Originally, she had been in route to meet with a scientist, and then meet with Brooke and Dragone not far from here, but she had stumbled upon a group of Ones that were going to wreak havoc on the innocent.

They thought to hide amongst the crowd. Victoria could detect the Ones by both visual inspection and by listening in carefully to the surrounding area. Not only was there a slight deformity—their eyes were visibly enlarged and some had their left pinkies angled—but Victoria could now listen for the white noise at a very high frequency that would alert her to the Ones' presence as well.

She had been honing her skills these last several months and her powers were very strong now. Jonathon, her great uncle, who was also the sometime leader of the Ones, had powers that Victoria could now match in many ways. Fundor, one of the original Ones, was fighting for control over the Ones, but Jonathon was stronger and smarter. The division caused weakness that the rebellion was quick to take advantage of.

Many months before, Victoria, then called Claire, had escaped the Ones' clutches, only to discover she was, the chosen one. The fate and destiny of humans were tied to the rebellion. Although most humans had no knowledge that the Ones even existed, or, for that matter, even that the rebellion existed; a fight for the right of humans not to go the way of the dinosaurs was taking place. As most people were working and living their lives with only the normal, everyday matters of concern, the rebellion had the added burden of protecting the human race.

Victoria and Trevor had joined forces and were finding new ways to undermine the Ones. In some ways, the technology of the Ones far outweighed the rebellion, but in other more substantial ways the rebellion outshined anything the Ones had to offer. The unity, determination, and steadfast approach that the humans brought to the table would win the day. The rebellion was becoming more sophisticated in all facets of their operation. Slowly, they were bringing a few trusted individuals in the government onboard.

She needed to draw the Ones outside of this holy gathering. These abominations had come here to maim and kill those who had gathered to pay their respects to their fallen leader. There was always a way to cover up their true natures and the blame would be put on a scapegoat picked from the crowd.

Walking toward the opening out onto the grounds, she hastened her pace. If she could get them to follow her to the open ground she could better manage the situation. As if sensing her resolve, they put their plan in motion.

A cry went up from the crowd that someone had a gun. Panic ensued and people started to run in all directions. People were being pushed down to the ground by the sheer mass of people trying to flee the area. Gun fire could be heard along with the many shrieks of terror.

More people would be injured by the crush of people, trampled. The Ones concentrated on inflicting the maximum amount of damage.

Victoria focused on an Ones she spotted on the veranda. She drew his attention and dared him to follow. He did to his regret. She positioned herself beside a line of Cypress trees and waited. Using a very strong form of mind control, she pulled him toward her relentlessly. He was then quickly dispatched to the Netherworld and Victoria wasted no time taking care of the second Ones as well.

She would not be able to get them all. They would effectively disappear within the crowd and regroup their efforts to acquire her.

An ear piercing yell went out. Turning her head, there was an elderly woman in a wheelchair that was out of control rolling down a long asphalt driveway. A man was screaming while running behind. Slightly pudgy, and seemingly out of shape, he was trying in vain to catch the chair. It had gathered momentum on the downward slope.

Victoria knew by the way the woman was panicking that she would not be able to stop the wheelchair. She concentrated on the wheelchair. She had only used psychokinesis thus far in a controlled environment and never anything so large or moving so fast.

It was harder than she imagined; she focused with all her powers forcing the wheelchair to slow down to a crawl, then come to a smooth stop. The man ran up beside the wheelchair trying to ascertain if the woman was unharmed.

The man told the woman, "It's a miracle, Josephine. It's a miracle."

The man and woman kept repeating it was a miracle. That it was impossible for the wheelchair to stop on an obvious decline. She was just happy she was able to stop it before the woman had sustained any injuries.

She had come here to meet with the scientist that had been working on understanding the new developments the Ones had implemented. Although the efforts of the rebellion were increasingly effective, she knew their new experiments would broaden the scope of their reach. Figuring out their next strategic move was of the highest priority. Ophelia, Octavia, and Acanthus, the elders, had advised Victoria to pursue this avenue.

Recently, the Ones had experimented with a virus that they had used to infect one of the rebellion's outposts. Several inhabitants had fallen ill, including one of the elders, Octavia. Octavia, a highly respected elder and advisor, steadily worsened until Dr. Holmes along with Dr. Oliver were able to come up with a vaccination that reversed the negative effects.

She had wanted to meet Dragone and Brooke not too far from here. She was overly anxious to see her cousin. She understood how Brooke must be feeling having recently went through a similar situation of her own not long ago.

She knew how difficult it would be for Brooke to believe what Dragone would tell her. It would be so far out there, so far out of her comfort zone to even entertain the notion that what he was saying could be true. Brooke was so grounded this would be such a blow to all the things she believed to be true. Brooke liked a routine and rarely deviated from her preconceived set of rules she lived by. But then again, she had accepted her destiny, and she was more than sure, Brooke would as well.

Now, however, she didn't want her cousin anywhere near here. She would relay a message to Dragone and redirect him to take a different route for Brooke's safety.

Chapter 13

About two hours later Dragone pulled off onto a dirt road that she hadn't even noticed from the main road. It was hidden well amongst the tree line that seemed to swallow them up almost immediately. The lane was so narrow that the trees were hitting the windows on both sides, but that didn't slow Dragone down.

After about three miles Dragone turned to the left and Brooke could finally see somewhere else other than just directly in front of her. The land seemed to fall away. It was rocky with huge boulders that lay on both the left and right sides. Narrow such that it wouldn't allow for two cars to be side by side which meant it was a very dangerous road, especially at the speed that Dragone was maintaining.

About a quarter mile ahead Brooke could see where the road forked. Dragone took the left fork and soon they were at the safe house.

It was in the middle of the forest so she imagined it would be hard to spot. She gingerly got out of the minivan. Her body was stiff from all the travel. She stretched and looked around while Dragone got out and looked around as well.

"I need to get the van in the garage. Do you want to stay out here?"

"Yes. I need some fresh air. But, I really don't see a garage anywhere?" She looked all around but couldn't see any signs of a garage. "Where's the garage?"

Dragone smiled. "Just watch."

He got in the minivan and moved it over to a stand of trees. She couldn't quite see all that he was doing but he had rolled down the window and was giving voice commands. Then an opening appeared before her very eyes and Dragone moved the van forward until she couldn't see him or the van anymore.

What the hell, these people are James Bond types. What have I gotten myself involved in? Brooke looked more carefully at the house then. There was something unusual about the roofline. She walked over to the tallest hill and walked up a little ways until she saw what exactly was so strange. The top of the roof was disguised with actual trees and bushes growing on it. From the sky it would look like part of the landscape, indistinguishable from the rest of the surroundings.

"Pretty amazing, huh?"

Brooke jumped in the air. "Don't do that! I didn't hear you. Where did you come from?"

"Over there." He pointed toward a stand of trees.

"Oh, right. I forgot you must have doors in the bushes as well."

He just smiled. "Come Brooke, we need to get out of sight."

They moved over to the stand of trees he had pointed toward where he gave a voice command in a language she had never heard before. A hidden steel door slid open that lay on the ground. She saw stairs that descended down into the earth. It was lit by tiny lights on both sides of the stairs. She followed Dragone and it was disconcerting to listen to the doorway slide back into place behind them.

She momentarily felt claustrophobic and felt slightly panicky. She turned around and saw the mini lights were turning off behind them as they descended farther into the earth. The stairs were short and wide. The little LED lights turned off the moment your foot stepped away. Her hands started to sweat and she was about to say something when Dragone stopped.

"Now we'll enter through here." There was a flat screen on the wall that was dark but came on as soon as Dragone put his face close to the device. It appeared to be registering his retinas or something similar. A door opened to his left and she forgot all about how he had managed that when she saw the room before her.

It was approximately forty by thirty feet with soaring wooden beams. The furnishings were sparse, yet exquisite. Rich textures and bold colors of red and orange made the whole space say, wow.

Dragone interrupted her thoughts when he said, "Do you want a cup of coffee? I need a cup. I'll make a cup for you as well, if you would like."

"Sure, that sounds wonderful to me."

She got comfortable while Dragone made some coffee and called to her it was ready. "I'll be right there in a minute," she had called back. It felt really weird calling to someone else that she was ready for coffee. It sounded so domesticated. Like she lived with Dragone and he was making coffee after a night of love making the morning after. She shook her head in denial at the thought.

She walked into the kitchen and got that heavenly whiff of freshly brewed coffee. She loved that smell. Until that moment she had never really understood that she associated the smell of coffee with being happy. Memories of happy times with her family, and later her mornings with her dog, Deebo, forever tied the smell of coffee with happiness. She figured that's why she always smiled when she got a whiff of the heavenly brew. They sat down on the kitchen chairs and talked over some points.

"How much further is it to our destination?"

"Oh, I'd say about another three to four days or so. The problem is trying to stay undetected."

"Right." Brooke was thinking along the lines that staying with Dragone and only Dragone another three to four days or so would be a testament to her will power to withstand Dragone's effect on her.

As she was thinking about it she glanced over at Dragone. *Don't look, don't look. Shit, I just had to look Brooke. He is gorgeous, there's just something special about him. Remember I'm only an assignment to him, nothing more. I need to get to Claire or Victoria, whoever she is now. I need answers and I need my family.* Abruptly, she scooted her chair back with that god awful loud shrill sound she so disliked. It sounded just like fingernails across a chalkboard. It never failed to make her spine convulse.

"I need some fresh air. Can I go outside and walk around for a bit?"

He looked at her different, sort of cocked his head to the side. "Sure."

He got up and walked around the counter to stand in front of Brooke. Instead of walking past her he paused in front her.

"Oh, hell." He leaned down and gently put his hands on her shoulders and brought her up off the chair.

"What are you doing? Dragone?"

He ignored her. He lowered his head and kissed her. Slowly at first, as he lingered on her mouth, taking his time with her, Brooke tried to reason with herself.

All her questions were blown to the four winds. As she kissed him back, she realized she wanted this man unlike any other man in her life. Somehow he was different from the rest.

With inhibitions brushed aside she raised up to touch his face. They looked into each other's eyes with that knowing look.

Dragone took his time. Resuming where he had left off, he kissed her slowly giving attention to her mouth in ways that had never seemed important before. He lingered, kissing every crevice, every curve. And when he had explored every exposed part, he demanded entrance to her mouth; shocked her with exquisite softness and yearning he was building inside her. He made every small move monumental.

She hadn't known what she was missing out on. That he could be so experienced to make the simple act of kissing, leaving her breathless and wanting more—was so deliciously amazing.

She tried to tell herself to slow down, to think things through. But she quickly told herself to shut up. After all, she could only focus on one thing right now, and that one thing was all Dragone.

They practically tore at each other's clothes. With buttons flying and seams stretched, she screamed his name as he lifted her up and onto the table. He proceeded to do things to her that seemed impossible and daring. His hands were anywhere and everywhere. He surrounded her world and brought her unspeakable pleasure. She, in turn, felt inexplicitly unencumbered by thoughts other than right here, right now, and she expressed her womanly sensual self to Dragone's surprise. They came together and the heavens echoed their names for all eternity.

After what seemed like hours of sweet, sweet torture, she drifted off to sleep in the huge bed. She lay in the crook of his arm, very comfortable and content.

She slept soundly for hours only to awaken and find Dragone gone. She didn't quite remember how she had gotten to this huge bed. Having been so focused on Dragone, she had barely noticed when he had carried her and gently laid her down in this bed.

She remembered the way he seemed to almost cherish her. She in turn had taken her time and paid attention to every small nuisance. She pleasured him well. She had never been so brazen before. Why she had felt so totally free to give and receive she wasn't quite sure. She was still riding the pleasure high and unable to clearly focus on much else beyond here and now.

Slowly, she sat up and looked around. Her clothes were nowhere to be seen. Thinking back, she remembered she had thrown them in various places in the kitchen in her haste to remove them. The need to be skin to skin had driven out all sensible thoughts. She blushed down to her roots just thinking about the things she had done with him, to him.

Feeling a bit awkward about walking around naked to retrieve them, she sat there trying to decide what to do. She really shouldn't feel shy at this point, she reminded herself. She had just been intimate with Dragone in ways she had never been with any other man. It was one thing during the heat of the moment, and another thing altogether afterwards.

With all the mounting questions of her decision to make love with Dragone, she wondered what had gotten into her. *What in the world possessed me to let Dragone do those things to me? He must think, oh god..., what must he be thinking about me?*

Walking into the room with coffee in his hands, he had a smile plastered all over his face. She wanted to crawl in a hole. She held the sheet up in front of her like a shield. The coffee was placed beside the bed and he made no fuss about the fact that he had nothing on. She looked away embarrassed.

"What? You're not embarrassed are you? I thought we had moved past that phase, beautiful."

He had a look of a Cheshire cat ready to lap up his milk.

She looked up sharply. "Just what *phase* are you referring to?"

He hadn't noticed the way she was sitting up straighter now. Her tone had changed as well.

"Well, now that we've been most intimate and all..."

It was then he looked down at Brooke. She didn't look like she felt as great as he did.

"What?" He raised his hands up and out for the full effect.

"Would you be so kind as to bring my clothes to me, please?" she said with a mightier than thou look about her.

Actually, she looked pissed. He practically sat on top on her as he sat on the bed. He wouldn't allow her to scoot over. Nor would he let her bring the sheet back up around her neck that had been forced down by the action.

"Listen Brooke, I don't know how to say pretty things. Hell, I guess I don't even know how to say things right most of the time. I had a wonderful time with you. In fact, I had the best time I've had in the last couple of years."

She stiffened visibly, incensed.

"I mean ever, ever Brooke—really." He looked closely at Brooke. "I'm really messing this up aren't I?"

"Yes." She yanked on the sheet and brought it back up to her neck.

"What I meant to say, is, thank you. Thank you for your trust and thank you for a wonderful time."

He thought she seemed to like that comment. He thought she seemed calmer now. He just needed to think. He didn't know how to talk to women. He was more of an Ones killer. Wooing wasn't up his alley. *She has a calmer, more peaceful look now.*

He kept his face strictly neutral, showing no signs of what he really felt. He leaned over and kissed her, then stood up. He walked out of the room and came back with her clothes. Although he had no shirt and was barefoot, he had put on his jeans. The fact that he had done so, to save her from further embarrassment, seemed to please her. He leaned down and gave her a brief kiss.

"There are fresh towels in the bathroom" he called as he walked away. Brooke didn't see the smug look of pure pleasure on his face.

"Thanks."

Taking a shower seemed to bring some normalcy back to her brain. *How does a girl become so stupid when a guy kisses her?* she thought. "Probably the same way a guy stops thinking when a girl kisses him," she muttered to herself. She shouldn't read too much into it she decided. She quickly dressed and brushed her teeth. Combing her hair, she thought about little, trying to act like everything was normal again.

She walked out of the bedroom and into the kitchen. Needing to remember that they each, mutually had needed and enjoyed one another—consenting adults, that's all, she walked up to the island and sat down on a stool. She looked at the kitchen counter top and blushed. The things they had done. She looked over at Dragone and saw he was watching her.

"I need some fresh air if you don't mind, Dragone."

"I would prefer you stay here."

"I would prefer to get some fresh air." Her eyes never left his, as she continued to stare.

He just stood there, assessing her. *What? Does he think he now has the right to boss me around? I'm my own person and no one tells me what to do.* Before she thought of what to do next, he spoke.

"Sure."

"I will let you out through the tunnel entrance. I need to come outside anyway to check on a few items. You have to stay in close proximity at all times, but I'll be close by if you need me. All you'll have to do is call out for me if you need anything, anything at all. Make sure you don't go too far, Brooke."

Great, she really wanted some privacy, but by the granite look on his face she knew better than to ask that he just stay inside the fortress.

"Fine, thanks, Dragone."

After checking the perimeter they headed outside.

"Remember not to go too far Brooke."

"Okay." She waved to him and turned, needing both space and time away from him.

Chapter 14

Dusk would be approaching soon and the sky was slowly starting to turn different shades of color in the late afternoon. As she waved to Dragone and moved off toward the welcoming last rays of sunlight, she sighed. Dabbled sunlight made its way through the trees giving off a sheen effect on the lower branches. It felt good to just walk and pretend she was on vacation with no worries.

The forest seemed less scary now that she had spent so much time in it. Actually, she had never spent this much time in the woods ever. The men, thugs, whatever they really were, definitely scared her, but not the forest. Here, beauty reigned.

All those books she had read about the tranquil, serene presence of the great outdoors were really true. Seeing documentaries on the History Channel about how Teddy Roosevelt had saved huge swatches of land and had named them as parks, gave her a greater appreciation seeing them up close and personal. It would have been a shame if so much land had disappeared for new housing, buildings, and shopping malls.

Pushing all negative thoughts aside, Brooke took a deep breath and looked out over the forest. It was beautiful. Never really giving the great outdoors much thought before, she had been thinking lately, she should appreciate a lot of things more. She had inadvertently, through her haste to become an antique dealer, taken many things for granted.

The leaves were just starting to change color and there was a nip in the air. She imagined squirrels were visibly getting fat for the anticipated winter ahead and birds were feasting on the berries just beginning to ripen on the trees and bushes. Brooke could even hear what she imagined were frogs calling to each other somewhere close by, not in the water but in the trees. It definitely sounded like they were in the trees. So many wondrous things to discover here—the forest was really quite astonishing if one took the time to listen.

It seemed to Brooke that throughout history, each person individually contributed to or created his or her own piece of the pie. The world needed more pieces of the pie to be worthwhile. The so called, pie, needed more goodness and a whole lot less rotten ingredients.

It wasn't just that there were so many bad people, but more likely than not, that they just weren't educated to respect, help, save, and preserve this piece of land and water, called Earth. They were conditioned from an early age to use and take; being on the top of the evolutionary rung made you somewhat arrogant.

The algae bloom, the humming bird's migratory path, the honey bees decline, the loss of habitat for all things living in the Amazon and beyond, were being strained by the ever increasing demands of the human race.

The extinction list continued to grow. Manmade disasters like oil spills and nuclear accidents were constant reminders that man held its fragile surroundings in its hands. Fracking, the process of getting natural gas, let companies put upwards of dozens of chemicals into the ground, and, perhaps, potentially finding its way into water sources, that she was sure, decades from now, would make her relations wonder what the hell had been wrong with her generation.

Sonar blasts were another, not so top secret device that was used by the military among others, to find oil deposits. Some conspiracy theorists said what the government is really looking for are the mermaids. Based on the reports of a few former NOAA scientists working at depths miles down, there were sightings of possible mermaids lurking in the waters. Unfortunately, the blasts killed hundreds, even thousands, of our mammals. With little known direct impact on the populace, it went unnoticed until hundreds of beached whales started showing up.

Extinction 101. From fracking to sonar blasts, oil spills to nuclear accidents; our highly intelligent innovative genius was killing our planet one species at a time.

Brooke wondered why the Ones had come here. Did they want the rich resources? Or, did they want to enslave the current occupiers of that top rung position? It was truly a horrifying thought. Did we even deserve to be at the top? Perhaps they would be better stewards of the planet. No, no that couldn't be, she told herself. The Ones were takers, users.

There were many people that were caring and compassionate. From environmentalists, to doctors and nurses, many good people were ready and willing to help others should disaster strike. At least her people, the humans, were perhaps misguided somewhat, but she was sure in the end, the will of the people to save the planet and all of its inhabitants, would prevail. It had to.

This situation would be remedied and she would resume her life and all would be good again. She was most definitely a half-full kind of girl. Breathing in deeply the sweet, sweet, smell of the fresh forest air, a peaceful feeling settled within her. She felt differently somehow now.

She came to a decision. She would pick one area of need and contribute as much time as she could spare, to make a difference. The problem she had in the past, she only thought big would make a difference. She didn't have time or funds to build a community center, manage a food bank, send used books to Africa, or set up a health clinic for the uninsured.

It was so easy to go about your life just being self-centered. She for one had a greater appreciation now, an eye opening experience, so to speak. Any small way would make a difference to those you helped. She would find something that fit her schedule. From afterschool tutoring, girl scouts or boy scouts, to welcoming home soldiers, or giving time at the local animal shelter, it would be welcomed by her peers. Perhaps, it might inspire more of her acquaintances to volunteer as well.

Brooke knew people came together in times of great need. All across this land when disaster struck, friends and family showed their strength. Be it a tornado, forest fire, or hurricane, hordes of people and resources would flock to their rescue. But in between those trying times, many people seemed to forget amidst the trials and tribulations called life.

Her life, in particular, was very demanding and stressful. Always needing to stay one step ahead, she was forever planning for the next quarter, next year's profits and where she would reinvest them, etc., etc., etc. There had been little time to contemplate the fate of the disappearing rainforest and the extinction of some the rarest flora known to man, that just might provide cures for many of the diseases that afflicted her species.

Saying that we only had one Earth, so we needed to respect it, was so cliché, but so true. It was unbelievably difficult to imagine how one individual could make a difference; to see the bigger picture, as it were, she never had. Funny how running for your life, being pursued by beings much more scary than the boogie man, put your life into perspective. More people needed to make the very most out of each day toward the greater good, and spend less time trying to stick it to the next guy.

The men Brooke had been in a relationship with thus far had always disappointed her in the end. Of course, she fully understood some of those issues she had to own, but, nonetheless, her ability to pick a winner was batting a big fat zero so far.

Early in her college years, she had dated Eric on and off for eight months. It had been a Wednesday, she remembered this because it was the day she was taking her dreaded final in Chemistry, when her friend Kim called and said she had taken her watch in for repair to the upscale jeweler, Princeton's. She immediately spotted Eric with a buddy of his looking at engagement rings. Now of course, she knew Eric's buddy might be the one purchasing an engagement ring but no matter how much she reminded herself of the fact, she fancied having grand notions of a huge wedding in June with her honeymoon in Maui. There would be three or four kids later in the picture along with a marriage made in heaven.

When Eric had called saying he needed to discuss something important over dinner, she had been so sure her fairytale was coming true. She arrived at an exclusive restaurant downtown, anxiously waiting what Eric would tell her. As she sat down she noticed a man dressed in a tux holding a violin close by. Joy had soared in her heart with Eric's thoughtfulness. As the man came near her table she still remembered her words, "Oh, Eric, you are the most thoughtful, sweet man, and I love you so."

She had smiled at the violinist as he approached; she had thanked the man for coming. He replied, "Why, thank you ma'am." He gave her a questioning look as he continued on to the next table over.

With her mouth hanging open, she quickly recovered and closed her mouth only to look at Eric in stupefied surprise. The beginnings of total humiliation were setting in and she knew the dream was gone. He had muttered something under his breath about women and PMS then he said, "You're acting really weird, Brooke. Are you okay?"

His important discussion had been to tell her that he had received a promotion and it would require a permanent move. There was no, "I love you and can't imagine moving without you Babe." No, "Would you marry me?" No, "I love you Brooke." He had simply wanted to inform her that he would be leaving in three weeks and would miss her. He asked if she would mind storing some of his belongings until he was able to return for a visit. That experience had left her hurting and wary.

After having been burned once she was much more cautious the next time around. Right before she graduated, she met a man named Jason. Jason was a newly hired lawyer, right out of college. His family was well connected and wealthy. They had seemed so perfect for each other. Their interests, likes and dislikes, all seemed to mesh. All her friends told her it was a match made in heaven. She had wanted to believe, so she did. The signs were there but she never opened Pandora's Box. This time it would work, she had told herself.

Ultimately, she had wanted a partnership, he had wanted a wife who would stay in the background and support his aspirations of becoming an influential politician. Although he thought it wonderful that she was graduating with honors, he did not want a wife that had her own plans.

She found out later that his father had had an investigator look into her background only to hit several walls. It was simply too risky to marry a woman who had a possible shaky background. Jason had confronted her with the findings, seemingly to give her a chance to fully disclose her family's background. He had explained he wanted her very badly but he was serious about becoming a politician. He had to know everything about her background before he could possibly commit to a more permanent relationship. Brooke had explained what he and his father could do with their so called information about her and where they could stick it.

Thankfully, she had learned a lot about herself from these failed relationships. There was no need, no rush, to be in a relationship with anyone. Strong of body and spirit, she could stand on her own. If, sometime, somewhere, she met a person whom she wished to share a lifetime with, well, she would make that decision when she crossed that bridge. And, so, she had been relationship free until she met Dragone. *Was* she in a relationship with Dragone?

Walking further along, totally oblivious to her surroundings, Dragone slowly filled her mind. He excited her, making her feel all woman, totally free to express herself. Never before, with any of her previous relationships, had she felt this sense of rightness. Like this was the one for her. Could it be that Dragone was her 'someone special,' the one she was destined to be with?

Brooke was an avid reader, from eBooks to hardbound, to magazines and periodicals; she couldn't read enough. In some previous books she had read, they described soul mates as that one true love that lasted a lifetime. Never having given it much credit, she had dismissed it outright. But, maybe you felt like this when you were truly in love with that special one. *Stop it, Brooke; you are trying to convince yourself a little too hard. He probably doesn't feel a thing for me, other than a really good time.* Nonetheless, she went back to thinking about what if, for another good ten minutes.

Life could be unexpectedly filled with happiness and tragedy. She knew that each of us were capable of loving more than one person in one's lifetime. One friend in particular, Leah, lost her dad when she was in college. By the time she had graduated, her mom was getting ready to remarry. Reportedly, her mom had loved her dad deeply and had fallen in love the second time around just as much. Who knew? Maybe, maybe Dragone was someone special too. Someone she could love a lifetime.

What happened? What happened that one day you could be unsure and the next you just knew that you loved someone? What made that On/Off switch move?

She didn't know what to make of him. There was a lot about him she still didn't know or understand and she wasn't sure that it mattered. Saving her butt, more than once, somewhat puzzled her. Not many people would have gone to all that trouble.

No matter what he said to the contrary, he cared, and he cared more than most. He was handsome, at least to her, and sexy as hell. His quirky smile emanated from his elusive character; it was somewhat of a mystery but promised a lot of spice. One thing she was sure of—he was one of the good guys. Not understanding him was frustrating, but he could be counted on to protect her from these so called Ones—of that, she was sure.

He was very complex. He was hard-headed, but gentle; forceful yet patient. *He would make an excellent father.* Where in the world had that thought come from? Remembering a little too late that she wasn't on the pill, and he hadn't used protection that she could remember.

Come on Brooke, how was I to know that I would be dragged through the forest and then would make maddening, mind blowing love to a man. The last time I was with any man was so long ago, that I should have read a book on the subject. Going for a walk in the park was apparently quite dangerous. She reminded herself she had bigger problems at the moment. Like the Ones looking for her.

Deep in her own thoughts, she walked for quite a distance. Not paying any attention to her surroundings until she realized Dragone would be furious with her. He had distinctly told her not to go too far. Granted, he hadn't specified what 'too far' meant, but she was pretty sure she had exceeded that quota. Everything seemed to be jumbled up in that brain of hers, and talking and walking was not helping that she could detect.

I just need some space dammit. Not only has the whole world gone crazy, but things with Dragone are moving way too fast. I need my damn life back, she screamed silently to the heavens.

She looked up, absorbing the last rays of the sun. The rays enveloped her and wrapped her in its warm embrace. She closed her eyes and felt, heard, and inhaled her surroundings. She stood still for several minutes just being. Nothing else—just being. It made her feel as if all her worries had been pushed off her shoulders down a steep slope. She immediately felt serene. It was enlightening and invigorating.

Not caring, she went about another quarter mile or so, until she thought better of her rash plan and intelligence seemed to return. She sat down on a nearby rock and really looked around. She needed to head back now that she had cleared her head of some of the cob webs. She knew the way she had come, so it wouldn't be very difficult. Or so, she had thought. Being honest with herself, she really wasn't all that good with directions.

Once, she had visited Washington, D.C. with a tour group. Deciding on a little alone time from the group, she had ventured out on her own. She had wanted to see Ford's Theater. That was where, then President Lincoln, had been assassinated.

The literature indicated it was on 10th Street. It should have been relatively easy to get off the subway at Metro Center and walk down G Street over to 10th. But not for Brooke; she had ended up at New York Avenue.

Feeling really inadequate, it had taken her twenty-five minutes to make her way back. Arriving at her hotel, she saw the tour guide pacing in the lobby. He had not been pleased when she explained her excuse for holding up the group.

She looked up in the sky and determined which way was west. That information really did very little because she really didn't know what direction it was back to the safe house. *Damn, damn, damn*, she thought. She should have paid better attention, darn it. She'd had her head in the clouds. She headed back east for no good reason other than it appealed to her.

As she walked back she noticed that the frogs didn't seem to be chirping anymore. Did frogs chirp, or was that just birds? In fact, she couldn't hear the birds either. Uh oh, that couldn't be good. She went several more steps before the hair on her arms stood up. Something was very wrong here.

As she looked around, the only cover she saw was a prickly bush. She lowered herself inside the prickly bush that looked lush and full of greenery. Silently she whispered, "Ouch, ouch, ouch." She stayed quiet for several minutes waiting. Waiting for what, exactly, she wasn't sure. Several minutes came and went; she was about to call herself silly and start back to the safe house, when, she heard a noise that seemed out of place with the rest of the forest sounds. She froze in place.

Two individuals wearing hoodies walked close enough that she could just make out the hoodies but she couldn't really see their faces, strange—very strange. Brooke didn't move a muscle. She wasn't even positive if she was bothering to breathe.

She could hear her heart racing, beating so hard, so loud, pounding as if trying to break out. The men would hear. They had to hear. If not, then they most assuredly would smell her fear. They stayed there for what seemed like hours, but, was really more like seconds, until they quietly left in the direction she had come.

Dragone is going to kill me for not listening to him. It was not a happy thought. Right now though, she needed to find a way back to Dragone—to safety. She now thought of Dragone as providing safety.

It was much better than the alternative, which was going with these individuals, these supposed Ones, and possibly finding out the hard way, just what, exactly, they wanted from her.

She was about to move out of her hiding place when she felt a push in her mind to stay put. A forceful push, but it was too late. She had already started to move when she saw the two hoodies approaching. The hoodies seemed to be filled with a vast amount of emptiness, dark, and evil. Looking straight into the hoodies as they approached, she saw nothing at all. She screamed as they came for her.

Chapter 15

That's all she could remember about yesterday. She had woken earlier but she continued to feign sleep until she could gather some information about her surroundings. With her eyes just barely open enough to see slightly, she could detect movement not far from where she laid. As best as she could make out she was lying on a small twin-size cot that was not about comfort. She was in some sort of cold sterile white room.

"I know you've woken, Brooke, so you might as well sit up."

Brooke tried not to react, but nonetheless, she felt small tremors throughout her body. She slowly sat up and looked around. The voice had come from a man sitting not very far away at a work station that housed all different kinds of devices and machines that looked very high tech to her. She didn't recognize even one instrument nearby.

He had on a white lab coat over top jeans and a polo shirt that was tucked in. He appeared to be in his early 30s with very fair skin sprinkled with freckles and bright red hair that needed taming. Brooke had never actually seen a pocket protector up close, but he had one in the breast pocket of his lab coat that was threatening to fall out because he had so many pens and pencils stuffed inside it. Although quite handsome, there was no smile on his face and no smile lines to indicate he ever smiled or laughed.

"If you even think about escape, or if you try anything out of hand, the guard just outside this room will bind you to the cot. You wouldn't want that, now would you?"

"No, I would not."

"Good. Then we understand each other perfectly."

"What do you want with me?"

"We will get to that. There is plenty of time for everything. You just do as I say and all will proceed as planned. I'm sorry about the bump on your head. My men got a little carried away."

She touched her head until she located a bump the size of a quarter. It hurt to just gently touch it. *So that's why I was unconscious.* Brooke had been praying that they hadn't done any experiments on her. Thank god all she had was a killer headache.

"I will require a blood sample if you're feeling up to it."

She shifted her body anxiously. "No. No, I don't believe I feel up to it quite yet."

"You misunderstand me. When I politely ask you, you will do so promptly and without question."

Brooke got up from the cot. He motioned for her to sit in a chair that had a covered tray beside it. He walked over and removed the covering. There were six vials waiting to be filled. Brooke looked around the room. There was a window in the door and she could see one guard looking in. She saw no other exit and no other possibilities for escape.

As he prepared to take her blood she thought about trying to fight her way out. "I wouldn't if I were you. You would not make it ten feet outside this room. There are many more guards and many more doors before you would reach the outside."

He continued to talk as if he were talking with an old friend about the upcoming holidays. "Tomorrow you will be given a full health assessment by our team before your transition into the breeding program."

Brooke exploded into action. She grabbed the needle from his hands just as she swung her fist and connected with his nose. He fell to the floor holding his nose. She picked up the lab tray dropping all the instruments to the floor and hit him on the side of the head as he tried to stand.

The door started to open; instinctively, she ran to it. She still had the tray in her hands. She swung the tray with all her might, but she was no match for the strength of the guard. The taller one simply grabbed the tray and backhanded her. The force with which he hit her sent her flying across the room. She sat dazed, sprawled on the floor, unable to get up.

The taller guard called over to the man in the lab coat still trying to stand. "Are you alright Dr. Hardy?" He motioned for the second guard to help him, as he was watching Brooke.

"Yes, I'm alright."

Slowly, getting to his feet with the aid of the guard, he wiped off the blood with his now ruined lab coat. He walked over to where she sat on the floor. He casually leaned over in order to get eye level, and slapped Brooke so hard she thought some teeth would fall out. Her head whipped back and to the side; she immediately registered pain in her neck and head. Her jaw was on fire.

"You will pay for breaking my nose, bitch. Tomorrow can't come soon enough for me." He started to rise. He appeared to have changed his mind and leaned back down to peer into Brookes' eyes. "Yes, I will enjoy this immensely." He slapped her once again, relishing the look of obvious pain she displayed.

She was hauled up by her hair by the guard and pulled by the hair to a holding cell. It sat in the middle of the room next door. It had bars all around and offered no privacy. It was about seven by nine feet with a small cot and a small bedside tray next to it.

The worker tables were situated around the cell where everyone could watch her. As she sat down she noticed all the workers were staring at her. Men and women, all with lab coats on, looking at her like she was the freak.

"You're the freaks!" she yelled.

They went back to working and pretending she wasn't there.

Chapter 16

The group of high profile money makers and shakers were here in Washington; gathered at the fundraiser tonight. The event would bring in hundreds of thousands for the advancement of the arts in schools across America. But there were other, not so noticeable, money making deals going on behind the scenes that had nothing to do with fundraising for a worthy cause.

The room was filled with people. Mingling and drinking, the crowd seemed jovial. Politicians, entertainers, socialites, and the like were working the social scene before the fundraiser got underway.

It was a grand ballroom, big enough to easily accommodate a couple hundred people or more. There were palatial Greek style columns situated throughout the ballroom along with settees and arm chairs, various sculptures and oil paintings.

One humongous all-stone fireplace that had a mantle the entire width, which was approximately twenty feet or so; it had obviously been hand carved to produce an intricately carved masterpiece, a one of a kind. It was at the far end of the room which had several love seats and plush chairs around it that encouraged you to sit.

Arched windows that practically ran the full height of the soaring ceilings were gorgeous. Lovely sheer drapes hung at their sides. A small orchestra played Beethoven's Symphony No. 9. The music was just loud enough to be moved by it but low enough to speak with each other. Vases filled with fragrant flowers were positioned throughout the ballroom. Chandeliers hung in the space as well as wall sconces. The overall effect was one aimed at wowing the guests.

General Peterson was among the crowd but he only *seemed* to be having a good time. He snapped his fingers to gain the attention of a nearby waitress who was carrying a tray full of drinks, and gestured for her to bring him a drink. He preferred Sherry, but decided on a Long Island Tea instead. As she walked away he thought about telling his man, Sherwin, that he wanted her at his home tomorrow sometime after three o'clock in the afternoon. He was just about to head in a different direction when he heard his name called out.

"Excuse me. General Peterson, sir. May I introduce to you my niece, Sohayla. She is a recent graduate of Yale University."

Turning he saw Mr. McDonald, a government employee at the Pentagon, approaching with a woman by his side that had curves and voluminous breasts, which he immediately wanted to know more intimately.

"Of course, it is my extreme pleasure to meet you, Sohayla." And it was. She was a looker. He looked at her long enough to take her all in, but not too long to offend. He briefly shook hands with both her and her uncle.

She had noticed his inappropriate appraisal but said nothing. "Thank you, it is my pleasure, I assure you, sir."

After exchanging the usual polite conversation, General Peterson excused himself and moved off in a different direction. He walked away having decided on a course of action to get her alone, and very soon.

Having met General Peterson, Sohayla seemed preoccupied with her thoughts. "Uncle, do go right ahead and greet your friends and colleagues. I see Colleen over there. I will go hang out for a while."

"Are you sure, Sohayla? I mean, I can easily forego these tiresome introductions if you want to leave. I have already introduced you to General Peterson, as you requested. I will submit your resume to his office personally next week."

"Thank you Uncle. No, you go ahead and enjoy yourself for a while. I want to catch up on some news with Colleen and mingle little."

"Okay. See you in a while honey."

Sohayla's uncle moved off toward a group of some of his friends he saw on the other side of the room. Sohayla meanwhile, headed in the direction of Colleen.

Calling out to her friend as she walked toward her, she couldn't help but stare at her attire. She had on a killer black dress with stiletto heels. "Hello, Colleen. How are you? You look amazing. I love that dress."

"Thank you. I found this dress at a vintage shop downtown."

Sohayla briefly spoke with Colleen. They exchanged information concerning their families, making a date to get together next month. She took advantage of the situation when a close friend of Colleen's, Sheila, came by to say hello.

After exchanging the usual small talk, she left promising to stay in touch. They would see each other at the upcoming baby shower for Ashton in three weeks. She made a quick note to self to go to Ashton's baby registry a.s.a.p. Making her way quickly now toward a back hallway, she slipped unnoticed into a backroom.

After the formal niceties that he was resigned to withstand, General Peterson moved away from the crowd down a darkened hallway. He opened a side room door where Dr. Hardy was waiting, pacing back and forth.

"I told you not to contact me unless it was extremely urgent."

"No one has seen me. I wish to remind you I was invited to this event. Relax. I will leave out the way I came. No one will know I was here," stated Dr. Hardy.

"Get on with it. What do you have to report? And…, it better be good for your sake."

Dr. Hardy just stared back at General Peterson. He wasn't the least bit intimidated. He was, after all, the chief scientist and researcher, in charge of all operations, or would be soon. He knew his worth quite well. General Peterson and his cronies were nothing without him. He, singlehandedly, had saved the Ones, time and again.

"Brooke has been acquired. She will be installed in our breeding program right away."

"That is excellent news. Yes, excellent news indeed. Has she been given the health assessment yet?"

"No, but she will be a match. Of this, I am sure. The health assessment will be given tomorrow afternoon."

Many humans could not tolerate the Ones blood in their systems. A small handful could not only tolerate the Ones blood flowing in their systems, but could regenerate as well. Some, like Brooke, could produce new Ones that were stronger than the originals that had come to this planet so long ago. Brooke, and those like her, had Ones blood running in their veins, but it remained undetectable to anyone looking.

"Very good." At this he implied their discussion was now over.

Dr. Hardy stood up. Dr. Hardy only obliged General Peterson because he wanted to leave, not because the pompous ass thought he should. He left out the side door where his limo was waiting.

General Peterson returned to the fundraiser. Plans were moving along nicely. Soon he would move to position himself for the possibility of being nominated for Secretary of the Department of Defense. The impending retirement of Secretary Wilson after only having served one year in office due to a sudden illness, would all but ensure General Peterson's nomination by the President. The Senate confirmation hearings would not be a problem. He already had several senators in his pocket.

It was most unfortunate about Secretary Wilson. He had a heart defect that was just recently discovered, shortly after his last surgery for gall bladder removal. Yes, all his plans were falling into place rather nicely.

Sohayla quietly, seamlessly, returned to the fundraiser. She pulled her prepaid cell out of her pocket. "Read synopsis for upcoming book. It's a winner." She hung up. As she walked by the women's restroom she deposited her cell in the trash can. On her heels was a janitor hired to keep the room clean, he began to empty out the can and put fresh trash bags in.

Continuing on, she grabbed a drink from the tray of a passing waiter and then she approached her uncle. "Are you ready, uncle dear? I must say, another one of those pesky migraines is coming on. Do you mind taking me home now?"

"Of course, my dear, just let me say goodbye to my good friend Tom." After exchanging goodbyes and well wishes, they left. The concierge got his Jag, and they headed home.

Chapter 17

Sitting there, Brooke thought about her situation. She was under lock and key, being watched by guards. The interior room was certainly secure, so she was quite sure the rest of security in this place was going to be tighter than she could fathom. Just how, was she going to get out of here? Trying to be discreet, she paid attention to everything going on around her. Maybe some small observation would lead to her figuring out a way, or means, to leave this place.

Clearly, the workers were doing some kind of research, but what? The tech closest to her looked to be in his early 40s. He had a white lab coat on like the others, and he was intently working, hunched over a work bench that had canisters sitting on top of it. The canisters were only about 12 inches high, but whatever were in those canisters were emitting some type of noise. The tech next to him was a woman with a full head of dark curls. She couldn't see her face but she guessed, she too, was in her 40s. All the techs were engrossed in their work. What the hell were they doing? And, how was it that noise was coming from those canisters?

Brooke saw several guys, Ones maybe, coming and going from the room toward the back. She noticed that a few seemed to have the same colored eyes and they seemed to have eyes slightly larger than usual.

There was definitely a storage facility of some type toward the rear. She had already seen a worker bring in some of the canisters, only to see them disappear inside a room that had a vault-sized heavy door. The door itself appeared to be at least two feet thick. It appeared to be made of some type of metal with black spaces on it. At first glance, it looked like deep impressions into the metal structure that created shadows, but with closer inspection it looked more like something black filling those deep depressions into the door itself.

In addition, the only people she actually saw coming and going from inside the room had special-ized clothing on. Not like scientists she had seen on documentaries or the like. These techs or scientists, whatever they were, had on dark blue scrubs that had black spots on them. The only other covering was on their faces, protecting, more specifically, their eyes. It was some kind of eye protection she had never seen before; somewhat like a pair of goggles, yet not. This eyewear had very wide sides that were black, sort of like the stuff she saw on the vault door.

While she was pondering over all this confusing information, a man dressed in a business suit that appeared to be an expensively tailored cut, walked into the room. Her eyes were drawn immediately to him. Being quite tall he seemed to dwarf everyone else in the room. He had graying hair along with those slightly larger eyes. *Very unusual,* she thought.

The techs scrambled to remove themselves out of his path, as if they were extremely wary of him. He didn't seem to waste so much as a glance on them. He walked purposefully, a slight gait to his walk, and came to a stop near a door off to the side she hadn't noticed before.

Dr. Hardy emerged from the door, as if on cue.

"I want her moved today to the east wing," said the man in the suit.

"I haven't finished with her yet, she is to be given a full health assessment before she can be moved. It's simply not possible," said Dr. Hardy.

"You question my authority in this matter?" the man in the suit said with his eyebrows raised questioningly. His words hung in the air; it was meant to be a threat as well as a question. His eyes never left Dr. Hardy. They assessed each other saying nothing.

The workers scrambled to get away from the two men as fast as they could move without bringing undo attention to themselves. Only one worker returned to his cubicle; the rest retreated to the back of the room under the pretense of gathering supplies.

"I do not question your authority Mr. Diefenbaker, I am simply overriding it."

This Mr. Diefenbaker glared at Dr. Hardy. He appeared to be extremely angry. Brooke thought the techs were smart to go to rear of the room. She wished she could too. Brooke was waiting for what was sure to come, but nothing happened. Mr. Diefenbaker abruptly turned and walked out of the room but not before he slammed his fist into the tech sitting in the cubicle close by. The tech made a sickening sob and fell onto the floor unconscious.

You could have heard a pin drop. No one dared to be the first to move.

Loudly, his footsteps could be heard, eerily slow, steady, and forceful. Dr. Hardy approached the cell with Brooke in it. With no other sounds in the room, he looked at her menacingly and said, "You will not leave this place unscathed. You will pay for the damage you caused today. I have plans for you Brooke; ... nasty ... evil ... plans for you, my dear." He had emphasized each word slowly for the maximum effect. It worked.

Brooke could not hide her reaction. Looking at him, she saw emptiness, a bottomless pit, with no feelings, no sense of right or wrong; just a pair of eyes that were cold and evil, if there was such a thing. His were eyes that never saw the beautiful, fragile and sweet. He never gave or received love. Never knew happiness. She could almost feel sorry for him—almost.

Imagining what he could truly be capable of, what those eyes of his revealed, she started to envision bad things. She couldn't help it; never before had she encountered such a man. He smiled when he sensed her fear. Immediately she knew he had been waiting, waiting for a sign of her fear. He fed off the fears of others; he found pleasure where there was pain. Turning, he casually walked away while whistling a tune. He was whistling, Yankee Doodle Dandy.

Brooke sat down hard on the cot. Her legs were shaky, like they couldn't support her weight. He was mad, madder than mad. He was the epitome of a scary evil scientist. What did he have planned for her? What was she going to do? How could she escape this madhouse? No matter what the consequences, she was now determined to leave this place one way or another. Chances were, she would probably have to find the first opportunity to fight to the death, as she knew now with certainty, death would probably be the best of all possible options.

The tech was removed from the room by two of the guards. They roughly grabbed his hands and feet, carrying him across the room. As they approached the door they dropped him on the floor, waiting for someone to hold the door open. The other techs observed the rough treatment along with the loud thud his head had made when they dropped him by the door.

After several minutes the techs resumed their work. Seeing that the guards had not yet returned, she spoke to no one in particular, "I see how they treat their workers, like disposable trash. You are only useful if you can perform. I bet no one will ever see him again."

The techs all looked at her then, seemed to hang on to each word. You could almost see the indecision, the doubt, the realization that, they, too, were disposable, replaceable. They stood there, just looking, thinking, when one of the guards came in.

He looked around, "What the hell are all you people doing? Get back to work."

One of the techs, although timid, spoke up, "Where did you guys take Don? Is he going to be okay?"

"Yeah, he's gonna be okay. As a matter of fact, he's already awake and talking to Dr. Hardy. He's decided to transfer to another lab that's closer to his home. I think he'll be in soon to clear his desk."

The workers went back to their tasks. An hour later, one of the guards came in and cleared out his personal belongings. The techs threw discreet glances at each other.

The moment the guard went out, Brooke said, "See, I told you. He will never be seen again. And, if you are found to no longer be useful, you will be gone forever too."

She looked up and saw one tech, a man in his 20s, looking at her with worry plain on his face. Everyone hurried to look down at their work except for this man. His hair was cropped, in complete disarray, and he had a serious acne problem. He was unkempt in appearance; his shirt looked as though it had been slept in with one shirt tail hanging out; his pants looked worse for the wear. Even his shoes needed a serious waxing.

He went past her on his way to his seat; quietly, she said just above a whisper, "If you are interested in helping me, I will help you. Someone will come soon to rescue me, and all disposable people will be, well, disposable. I can make sure you aren't one of those people." She had purposely looked only at the ground so as not to draw any attention to her.

He sat down and pretended to work on one of the canisters. "What do you want help with?"

Excitement filled her. "I need the security system to be down."

"Are you crazy? The monitoring room is secure. I could never get in there."

"I bet you're a computer genius."

"Yes, but what does that have to do with it?"

"You could hack into their computer. I only need a little time."

He said nothing for a few minutes. Brooke understood the odds against escape. She had to have help from someone. Maybe one of the other techs could be persuaded. Then, he spoke.

"You'd help me get away from these guys?"

"Yes."

"I'll think about it."

For rest of the day he didn't so much as look her way. Time was running out.

As she sat there contemplating what, if any, other options she had over looked, when she noticed a courier had entered carrying several boxes on a hand truck. He gave her an off-handed glance as though he was surprised to see anyone in the cell and then looked away quickly. The lab tech nearest her cell waved the courier over to him.

They both had their backs to her. That is why they didn't notice a small piece of paper that had been on the side of the bundle fall off the stack and gingerly float forward only to land inside her cell. She casually walked over and after glancing around to make sure no one was paying attention to her, she picked it up. After balling it in her hand, she took her time stuffing it inside her pants pocket.

The courier finished the delivery and left. He glanced once more toward Brooke as he left.

She was dying to take a look at the shipping label and order summary, but couldn't for fear someone would see her. About an hour went by as she worked up the nerve to ask a nearby technician if she could be allowed to visit the ladies room. Fifteen minutes later, a huge guard, who looked very put out by the interruption, opened the door and motioned for her to follow. He led her to the back of the room. The bathroom was tiny with two stalls within. She took care of business first and then quickly retrieved the piece of paper she had so carefully put in her pocket.

It was a bill of sale from a laboratory in Santa Monica.

It had a very lengthy list, all of which she couldn't even begin to pronounce, let alone know what they were. Names like, Maitotoxin, Quinine, Lysine, Indium, Gallium, and Thallium. She put it in her bra for safe keeping and quickly washed her hands.

A loud sound, much like an explosion, let her know the guard was there. He threw the door back knocking it roughly against the wall, causing a sizable dent in the sheet rock, staring at her. "Let's go. You've taken long enough." He grabbed her by the arm, so forcefully, that the pain made her wince. Before she could attempt to pry his fingers off her arm, he practically threw her across the room.

With her good sense somewhere else, she turned and spit in his face. "You pig. You …" before she could utter another syllable he had back-handed her with such force blood started pouring from her lips. They were both split, her top and bottom lips, her head was reeling, and the guard was cursing at her.

"God damned bitch. Get back in the john, clean yourself up. Now! Or, so help me." He raised his hand again just as another guard appeared.

"What the hell happened here, man? You better get her cleaned up and fast. I'm not taking the fall for you; if Dr. Hardy sees this, you're toast. Shit, man. I'll have to report this."

"No, you won't. She'll be back in her cell in five minutes—won't you bitch?" He looked over at Brooke.

She didn't move, she was thinking about doing one more stupid act. She gauged she just might be able to poke his eyes and grab his gun. She wanted very badly to hurt him and teach him a lesson he soon wouldn't forget. She passionately disliked people who bullied or abused others.

He caught her in the middle of her thoughts, when he slapped her across the face for emphasis. Getting right in her face with his spit flying in her face, he said, "you better get in there and clean up real good or I will take you back and do it for you. And.., maybe I'll just decide to give myself a little bonus while I'm in there." Stepping back, he looked her up and down, as if trying to decide.

She was almost ashamed, when she cringed and cowered away from him. Moving swiftly to do his bidding she hid her tears. Entering the rest room she was shaking; she tried to pull some paper towels down from the dispenser so she could wipe some blood from her clothes. She managed to get a few down, then throwing water from the basin all over her face, she jerkily stood up.

Looking in the mirror, she saw a very different Brooke before her. Her eyes were puffy, her lips swollen and cut, a hand print was visible running along the side of her cheek. She looked beaten down, mentally as well as physically. So this was what it was like to be abused. How demeaning and soul draining; her empathy for so many abused victims, instantaneous.

She berated herself, tried to gather energy, to not to be afraid of him. She should have kicked his ass, but she couldn't; he was meaner, tougher, and he had the gun. She hated the bastard.

Chapter 18

As she returned to her cell, everyone was staring at her. Tears had stained her face. She was sure she looked like hell. She be damned if she would cry in front of these people. She wasn't so sure that they were there willingly, so she guessed she shouldn't be judging them, but why didn't they do something? Get help; tell someone, something, or anything.

Her head was killing her. She could feel the swelling in her lips. It was hard to keep her lips closed. The throbbing on her face was painful. She could literally feel the hand print on her cheek as if he was standing there pressing his hand against her.

Pain lanced her brain, robbing her ability to think clearly, and focus was what she needed to be doing right now. Someone would come soon, very soon to rescue her. Who was she kidding? No one knew where she was; let alone looking for her, except for maybe Dragone. He had no way of knowing where she was; she would have to figure this one out on her own.

She glanced over at the tech, the one who had talked to her. Looking around, everyone seemed engrossed in those canisters. She took a chance, quietly she said, "Hey, do you want to help me or not? A small army will be here soon to help me escape. I can make sure you get out of here alive."

The tech replied, "I'll think about it." He got up and walked away.

She couldn't wait around for this guy. She saw another tech close to her on the other side of the cell. Under the pretense of stretching, she walked to the other side of the cot. Deciding it was now or never, she tried to speak to her. Speaking softly she said, "I know for a fact, a small army will be here soon to get me out. If you would like to join us, let me know now."

The tech turned her way then back toward her work. Ten minutes later, she said quietly, "I want to leave this place but I'm afraid."

Brooke had to strain to hear her, she spoke so softly. "I need help. Do you think you could get me a gun or a knife?" She said nothing for so long, Brooke was positive she wouldn't get any help at all.

Whispering the woman said, "I can try. The last two days the guards have not checked my bag."

"Thanks. I…" Just then the guard that had hit her came in. He walked over to the cell Brooke was being held in. She couldn't help it; she purposely looked the other way, refusing to look at him.

He stood there for a second or two, and then moved off in the direction of the storage facility. She hadn't realized she'd been holding her breath; she let it out slowly, shaking all over again.

When she thought it was clear to talk again she said, "I cannot wait until tomorrow, it has to be today."

The woman got up and walked to the back of the room to collect a few canisters. She returned to her work area. Not a word was uttered for at least fifteen minutes. Brooke was anxious, silently pleading for the woman to agree. When she walked out of the door, Brooke was positive her last hope had just walked out the door with her.

Dejected, and feeling somewhat helpless, she tried in vain to come up with another plan of escape. Her intuition told her that more horrible things would be coming if she didn't find a way out.

The other techs were too far from her to try to speak to any of them without everyone being aware. Maybe, she could catch one of them as they walked by. It seemed the remaining techs in the room were determined not to walk near her cell. Going the extra steps to circumvent the path to her cell, they all went the long way around.

A short while later she saw the woman reappear with a drink in her hands from Arby's. Brooke was elated when she first walked in. Noticing right away something was amiss, her elation turned to dread.

The woman was sweating and she was nervous. Brooke was worried someone else would notice the woman's agitated state. The woman lost hold of her handbag and both the handbag and her bag of food fell to the floor. She quickly retrieved her handbag and set it on the desk. Part of her order of fries had spilled to the floor and she nervously picked them up. She didn't seem coordinated enough to scoop them up; instead she picked each one up one at a time.

Brooke could only look on with trepidation. Hope that no one would notice. *She must have something in her purse. Please, please just give it to me.*

Finally sitting down, she drank her Coke, with her back to Brooke, and ate her roast beef sandwich and fries. Brooke sat quietly but the anticipation was driving her crazy. Surely, she had went out and brought a weapon back in with her.

A guard appeared and walked up to the woman. "Angie, Mr. Bridges would like a word with you."

Muttering, she said, "Why, why does Mr. Bridges want a word with me? I haven't done anything."

He bellowed, "Do I look like a mind reader? How the hell should I know? And…, why do I care?" Standing there arms extended out, he was menacing looking as he towered over Angie.

"I need to use the Ladies Room. Please?"

"Whatever."

Getting up she did a quick glance Brooke's way, then proceeded to walk to the Ladies Room with her handbag with her. The guard was right behind her. When she emerged from the Ladies Room she still had her handbag with her. Brooke had a very bad feeling about this.

At least thirty to forty minutes came and went with no return of Angie. Extremely worried what Angie may have brought back in her purse, she was praying that she didn't get caught.

A couple of guards making their rounds came in the room, but no Angie. If only she could ask someone. The tech she had initially solicited help from was not even glancing her way. He was stoically sitting upright and quiet.

One guard stopped in front of the Ladies Room. He opened the door and was gone for about two minutes. He came out and disappeared out the door. No one in the room looked in his direction.

This is so not good, thought Brooke.

Two doors down, the room was not so quiet. Angie had been questioned about the reasons behind bringing a small pistol into the building. It was a NAA Guardian Pistol built specifically for ladies. The guard had found it inside the paper towel dispenser in the Ladies Room.

Mr. Bridges had most definitely noticed her erratic behavior entering the building. He had monitored her as she was able to bypass the guards without a bag inspection and then watched her make her way down the hallway. The guard in question would no longer be employed there or anywhere for that matter.

Under interrogation, she said she only remembered she had brought the gun in with her after entering the building. Upon which time she didn't know what to do. She said she was selling the gun for financial reasons. She had meant to leave it in the glove compartment. She had been running late coming back from lunch and had forgotten that she didn't remove it from her purse.

Mr. Bridges didn't believe her. It had only taken removing one fingernail until her tune had changed. "Angie, if you tell me the whole truth I will tell Johnny here to stop hurting you."

Angie pleaded, "p plea ease, p please." The crying was preventing her from speaking clearly. Blood was now oozing from her left forefinger. The pain was excruciating to say the least. The man, Johnny, slapped her each time it looked like she was going to faint.

"The woman—the woman in the cell told me she would help me when a small army comes for her. I just wanted to go back to my quiet life. That's all. I didn't want to hurt anyone here, I swear. Please—just don't hurt me anymore, please." She was weeping, whimpering.

Mr. Bridges moved toward the door. "You really believed her Angie?" He looked over at Johnny, "Johnny, make sure she suffers."

"You said if I told you the truth you would stop hurting me," wailed Angie.

"And you believed me?" Mr. Bridges walked out the door.

Chapter 19

After a boring fundraiser, General Peterson was finally in his limo headed toward his townhouse in Georgetown. He looked out into the darkened streets of D.C. It was a beautiful city he'd have to admit. There were no such beauties on MAB13. MAB13 was the home planet of the Ones that was 13.3 billion light years away. They crossed over the 14th Street Bridge, as his driver hastened past both the Jefferson and Lincoln memorials on the way to Georgetown.

Ahhh, the Tidal Basin view. He never grew tired of it. Having no trees back on MAB13, the Japanese Cherry trees looked expressive even without blossoms. His driver knew to take this route on the way home. He thought he would keep it nice like this once the Ones were installed to their rightful station. As he sat back and enjoyed the view, he had a glass of sherry to celebrate. Soon, very soon, it would be his.

At home in the pool room he enjoyed another glass of sherry looking over his vast collection of art.

He surrounded himself with luxuries and exquisite art. He deserved the best, and demanded it. Studying his Koi fish, he decided which one he would feed to his piranhas. The one with the long blue vein, he thought. He would watch it wiggle at first, then watch as it would be torn, ripped and shredded to pieces, as the piranhas enjoyed their tasty treat. He had his Koi restocked monthly just for this pleasure. His man, Sherwin, knocked on the door.

"Enter."

"Sir, there has been another sighting. At 2100 PST there was a Level 5 sighting. It was reported and signed off."

"Is that all?"

"Yes sir."

"Be gone."

"Yes sir."

As Sherwin exited the room, General Peterson contemplated his options. With his connections through the Pentagon, he made sure he knew of all alien sightings. There was little he could do if contact was made. But he doubted it. They were too humane, too resided to the present situation. They would have contacted some government agency by now if it had been their intent. They wouldn't dare interfere at this late stage. No, they were only monitoring things for a historical prospective. They couldn't touch them on this planet, not now. Not when all their plans were coming to fruition. They mustn't. He just needed a little more time. And, when all was ready, even the Ones could not hide.

They had been served their punishment and had survived. His greatest desire other than taking over Earth was to wipe out every living being on the planet of MAB13. That too, would one day come, he reassured himself.

Perhaps he would need to step up his plans. The time table could be moved forward, but not too fast. That had risks. He called Sherwin and directed him to send for Dr. Goli as soon as the press conference was finished.

As Sherwin quickly moved to do his bidding, he turned the television on to CNP News. Christy Dillon, a news reporter, was speaking out about the global shortage of water and its overall effect moving forward. She was well spoken, a serious reporter, who had won numerous awards. Ms. Dillon was also an Ones—one of the best of the best, as far as General Peterson was concerned. Of course, no one matched his intellect, his brilliant strategic skills, etc., etcetera. She was, however, an asset to their cause. She was magnificent in manipulating her stories to always end with speculation, be it to instigate the beginnings of unrest, or instill the fear factor. She didn't oversell the fear factor because she didn't want to draw too much attention to herself. Masterfully, she had crafted her skills; the people loved her and followed her almost like a cult.

Yes, his well laid plans were all falling into place. The press conference was due to begin in fifteen minutes.

Dr. Goli was part of the program at the National Institutes of Health (NIH). On the surface, Dr. Goli's team was being credited with discovering a cure for the common cold for the age group 18-35. It was hoped that a new version, one for children and one for adults over the age of 35, would become available in the near future. Dr. Goli's team of researchers was secretly making a new, tainted formula that would be a testing ground for the Ones.

They would begin mass producing and releasing it to the population through their network of pharmaceutical companies within two years. This time table needed to be moved forward by at least one year now with the recent sightings of the Ones. They had two formulas, one for the cure of the common cold and another one that would be moved to a specific geographical location in place of the cure for the common cold. It would mean valuable collection of data. Dr. Goli would oversee this secret project until its completion.

He also had a team working at the Centers for Disease Control and Prevention (CDC). They had been pushing for the need of this new vaccination for every young person between the ages of 18 to 35. It was ground breaking, and everyone was onboard to get it to the market as soon as possible. One little annoying detail was that the U.S. Food and Drug Administration (FDA) had not signed off on it yet. However, he was sure his people would take care of that little problem very soon.

The team of researchers at NIH and CDC along with other governmental agencies' input had seemingly found the right application for the prevention of the common cold. It was all the buzz. Companies were scrambling to buddy up to Dr. Goli in hopes of being awarded the contract to mass produce it.

His man, Sherwin, came in.

"Sir, it is time."

He turned and exited the room. General Peterson changed the channel. It was about to begin.

Dr. Goli was seated at a long covered table with several doctors seated to her right and left. Microphones were positioned in front of each person along with a bottle of water. Reporters sat a few feet away. A reporter started the proceedings with the first question.

"Please tell us, what, exactly, has your organization discovered, Dr. Goli."

"Today, I present to the world a culmination of hundreds of thousands of man hours, the end result being a cure…" at this point a hushed silence broke out in the crowd, expectant faces, glued to the face of Dr. Goli, you could almost *feel* electricity all around you, "…for the common cold, age group 18 to 35. There is much anticipation that a cure for other age groups are close at hand."

The excitement was palpable throughout the gathered participants. Hushed murmurs could be heard all around the room. Dr. Goli let the other doctors on her team answer several questions. Twenty-five minutes later she stood, signaling to the other doctors she was finished, saying that another press conference would be organized for later in the week. With that said, the microphones were abruptly turned off and Dr. Goli exited the room.

Back in the news studio, the news anchor read from her script. "To recap, the National Institutes of Health (NIH), in conjunction with the Centers for Disease Control and Prevention (CDC), have found a cure for the common cold for the age group 18 to 35. Dr. Goli, being the lead researcher, has worked extensively for over 10 years on this project before this breakthrough was achieved. Having achieved numerous distinguished awards, including the National Medal of Science, Dr. Goli has had a long and productive career. In her earlier years as a researcher, she was the youngest woman to receive the American Society for Cell Biology (WICB) Junior Award.

The reporter continued speaking but General Peterson had heard enough. His plans were falling into place. He simply would not tolerate any interference.

His private line rang. "Yes. Five o'clock today." He hung up. Dr. Goli was on her way.

Dr. Goli arrived at 4:55 p.m. It was not advisable to arrive late at General Peterson's residence. She had been summoned and she understood her position. Although she thought of herself as superior and irreplaceable, certain members of the Ones actually had the audacity to think they were better than her. She was merely bidding her time, until the vaccination was firmly entrenched into the population. When all was in place, she would demand her rightful place at the helm of the new order, as she liked to call it, for they would be lost without her genius.

Going through two security check points, she waited in the foyer for General Peterson's man, Sherwin, to announce that she had arrived. Looking around, she decided she liked his taste in furnishings. She too, would have something like this mansion, soon, very soon. Perhaps in Bethesda, she liked Bethesda; or, perhaps Potomac. It would have to be grandeur and elegant, with a baby grand piano in a room filled with glass windows overlooking an in-ground pool with Jacuzzi and waterfalls.

In General Peterson's foyer there were two chairs that resembled chairs fit for a king. A slim desk with a portrait of the white house sat above it. The hardwood floors were a rich Mahogany; the Persian rug that sat on top had woven silk threads that mesmerized you. The chandelier hung like a cascading waterfall of crystal, probably from Tiffany & Co. at least twenty feet above her head.

This is why she had worked so hard. Dr. Goli was a genius and she would have it all, and soon.

General Peterson watched Dr. Goli enter. She was not attractive, but he thought she looked decent enough for a doctor. Not his type at all, but he supposed she was very useful for his purposes.

"Welcome, Dr. Goli. I want a full report on my desk in the morning concerning the latest research about the vaccination we will be launching soon. In addition, I want to step up the long term plans by a full year."

"Excuse me, General Peterson, sir. Did you say step up the long term plans by a full year?"

"You heard me, Dr. Goli. Is there a problem?"

"Yes sir, there is. I cannot possibly abide by that directive. It is quite impossible sir."

"You will make it happen, Dr. Goli. You will return to your lab, and direct everyone to step it up. Are we clear about this, Dr. Goli? I do not wish to repeat myself."

"Yes sir. I understand completely, sir."

"Good. We are finished here. You may take your leave."

He watched her stand and walk toward the door. "By the way Dr. Goli, how is your sister doing these days?"

Dr. Goli froze; she didn't turn around to give him the satisfaction of seeing her look of astonishment. She had hid her sister away; somewhere she was sure no one could find her. Her sister, rather her half-sister, had a disorder that the Ones didn't deem necessarily a threat but didn't think there was much value in her staying alive. Jessica had cerebral palsy.

"She is doing fine, thank you for asking."

"That's nice Dr. Goli. Goodbye."

As soon as she got in the car she punched in a number she had never called before.

"Hello." A strange voice answered from the other end.

"Hello, who is this?" demanded Dr. Goli.

"Never fear Dr. Goli, I will just stay here and watch over your sister for you until your operations are complete. Then, you can come here for a visit and see for yourself that Jessica is fine." The phone line went dead.

She had plans for General Peterson. He would regret the day he messed with her.

Chapter 20

This spacecraft was specifically designed for the extraction and experimentation of the mixed breeds. Yet again, they came.

The Ones commander, Xen, had received data on the latest mixed breed they had picked up for observation. The specimen in question had a tumor growing on the left side of his brain. A thorough examination additionally found the subject had trauma to the liver and spleen from an unknown source. Subject was deposited in location nearest original pick up point when examination was complete.

There had been many subjects such as this one. With some, there were more lasting effects of the experiments for those that could remember. Some humans, having gone through hypnosis, were able to grasp snippets of the experiments that had been performed. Sometimes they were able to recall and retain the memories extracted from years before. Hypnotists were not valued by the humans as a credible profession. They were discredited and the sessions were generally deemed staged by the populace at large.

They came in order to observe how far the Ones' advancements had taken place. Humans had told stories of alien abductions for decades but had been ignored for the most part, condemned as crazy hoaxes. And so, they visited on a fairly routine basis with little to no interference.

Several governments knew of their existence. Unconfirmed sightings were the norm since their inception. In secret, governments were devising platforms that encouraged aliens to contact them directly.

The SEC project (Space, Earth, Communication), the brainchild of the United States, had recently been implemented, and was situated in a locale known as Howland Island. It had multiple black holes with which they sent out messages to space. Black holes were from a material first discovered by explorers in the Arctic region. This unique metal found miles below the surface of the planet attracted other certain properties to it naturally. Eventually, the scientists found tuning abilities beyond their comprehension. Within two decades' time they were able to use this material across a broad spectrum of frequencies in secret.

Although the humans had developed techno-
logical advances in leaps and bounds over the last
several decades, they were still their own worst
enemy. Having no central power figure, the humans
repeated their mistakes many times over, to the
detriment of the planet as a whole.

One country treasured their resources while
another raped it. One region of the world constantly
fought with another. Civil wars were prominent
among the human population; they lacked the
understanding of a global community. The humans
had examples of cooperation that were plentiful all
around them in nature. It was noted that humans
preferred separatism, each, individually, seemingly
separate from the other, with no common ground
rules that they were governed by.

Having no other possible short-term viable plan
for resources, the humans showed little remorse in
using it up, with little understanding of the ramifications. Their engineers and architects pillaged, while
their designers and mathematicians plunged their
society into chaos with their meager attempts at
progress. The human progress stamped out anyone
or anything in the way—foolish humans. Xen knew
that in the archaic times of his people, eons and eons
ago, there had been recordings of such mentality

among his ancestors. Being superior in nature, they had overcome and endured.

There was precious little water on MAB13. Here, the humans only reacted to the dire shortage of water when it stopped flowing into the upscale neighborhoods, offices, and the farmer's fields; only when there was an immediate danger. Planners of their communities wiped the land of sustainability on an alarming scale. The humans showed promise intellectually, but before they would be able to accomplish all that needed to be done, they would more than likely destroy their only home.

Having stopped at Mt Kailash first, they then journeyed on to the geographic location known as Area 51. It was the wormhole the Ones had used as their original entry point.

The Ones, part of a group that had generated crimes so heinous against their kind, had been cast adrift and left without resources to die. They had somehow survived. Ultimately, they reached this planet, Earth, where it was to be discovered their powers greatly exceeded the current species.

As they discovered how to blend in, so to speak, they had begun experimenting with breeding possi-bilities. Their power and intellect, having been vastly superior, was no match for the humans.

It was determined the experiments by the deviate expats on the humans, were becoming more sophisticated. They had advanced greatly in their gene therapy and all indications were that they would be able to successfully breed and thrive. They had used a form of DNA mutation called, Frameshift. The Ones had perfected this technique along with Deletion DNA mutation as well. Some of the earlier mixed breeds had a DNA mutation called, Substitution. The scientists changed a different amino acid and caused a small change in the protein produced.

Somehow, they had produced a deficiency that not only caused a rare brain disorder, but this disorder was nearly undetectable. Using Somatic mutations, they experimented relentlessly on many subjects at their various lab locations. Although the mutations could not be passed onto the offspring, the Ones were changing all known existing research.

The Ones developed a new master gene that was accepted by the human body and could manipulate the functions it wanted to direct. Using the master control gene, they were able to take care of the problem the Ones had with their eyes.

They had also begun hydrogen testing. It was an old concept but the resources of the Ones were limited here. They had storage of various arms in many locations.

There were weaknesses in the Ones. Their longevity here on Earth was far shorter than their kind experienced on MAB13. It was unclear if the mixed breeds or the original Ones themselves, or both, had this flaw. Manmade environmental factors were thought to be one of the culprits.

The Ones found out that there were differing results depending on the use of certain types of people. African descent or European ancestry, for example, meant different results because their genetic makeup gave varying final results. So, the earlier versions of mixed breeds had their problems.

The human race was becoming a land of mixed breeds. The humans, other than a very small percentage, had no idea what was taking place on Earth right under their noses. The samples that had been gathered over the last century clearly showed the Ones' influence, beginning with some mixed breeds let loose on the Midwestern states in the United States of America.

Instigators and sometime murderers fanned out across America putting their mark on the land. As more began to emerge as rapists, bank robbers, mercenaries, and the like, the Ones realized these throwaways were instrumental to their cause. The Ones continued to experiment with and cast out their imperfections to the unsuspecting world at large. Russia, Germany, Australia, nearly every country, every region, now had some mixed breeds in their midst.

Upon examination of some of the mixed breeds the pinky finger on the left hand of the earlier subjects had a distinctive angle that was visible. Likewise, some subjects displayed slightly larger eyes than the average human had. This difference was slight and nearly undetectable by the average human. Although human blood tests would not reveal any abnormalities, a brain scan would.

Previously collected data indicated that specimen number 13245, showed signs of mental instability and had committed various crimes that had ended in said individual being hanged by the neck until dead.

Specimen number 13294 had started an insurrection in England that was quickly squelched but nonetheless ended in several deaths.

Specimen number 13301 had assassinated President Abraham Lincoln in Washington, D.C. in 1865.

More recently, Specimen numbers 13111 and 13567 had wreaked havoc across the Middle East instigating insurrection and profiting from the sale of arms to the highest bidder.

Xen was in charge of making a determination if the Ones' mixed breeds indicated a need to cleanse the Earth of all substandard species. What would the fate of humanity be? Would these mixed breeds possibly be a threat to their kind in the future? How long would it take for the Ones to fully take control over the populace? The fate of his ex-countrymen here on Earth would be decided as well.

Xen was fully engaged in his Tong activity when second in command, Sulvax, approached. Tong, was a mind game one participated in with multiple players. Joining others along the mental path that they were all connected to on their home planet allowed Xen to stimulate his skills while gone; eleven other Ones were participating today. Xen joined Zugar and Pehz in using their combined forces to squash the competition. In this virtual reality setting, the players would use pulsating impulses to bleed the intellectual side and enhance the aggressive forces, causing opposing team members to fight back in such a way that when they left their virtual reality, consequences could range from broken members, organ malfunctions, or degradation of intellect. Thanking his brethren for winning today, he signed off with satisfaction.

"Speak," remarked Xen.

"Sir, if I may, a large group of our expats, is currently engaged with the rebellion."

"Keep me updated."

"Yes sir."

Indications were that there was a power struggle between two Ones. One was purported to be a mixed breed. Indeed, a significant discovery. The strength and intellect of the mixed breeds showed advancements unheard of and groundbreaking.

There were rumors among the council members that they may initiate a program to continue experimentation with the human race for possible strengths and weaknesses that could further their own race. A wealth of data was being currently collected and evaluated.

Xen would not engage the Ones, but simply continue to gather data and make a final recommendation to the supreme leader of their kind.

Chapter 21

Dr. Hardy was a genius. His aptitude was unsurpassed in his field. Unfortunately, the world at large did not know about him as of yet, of his greatness, but he would remedy that fact soon enough. Soon there would be wonder and awe when his name was spoken. The Ones would speak of his genius for centuries to come.

He had single handedly ensured the survival of his species—little did the humans know about them. In fact, only a handful of the rebels knew the full story of how they came to be.

He was tired of letting the humans think they were in control. They actually thought they ruled this Earth, when they were, just a species that would soon be no more. It would take very little time to push their species close to extinction, as they had done to so many of the known species that had existed here for thousands of years. This time thou, they would be next in line.

His peers demanded secrecy until the appropriate time. He wanted to change that time table—and he would. His latest breakthrough would move his plans forward. He intended to use his newest discovery on Brooke without the approval of the almighty council, or whatever the hell they called themselves now. He didn't have time for their stupid meetings, or their rules, or their threats to try to keep him in line. They were all fools and he would soon have them regretting they ever questioned his abilities by not showing him the proper respect one so gifted should receive.

Many of the earlier mixed breeds he had experimented on had been failures in the eyes of his contemporaries. They were all ignoramuses. In fact, these had just been the missteps that had led him toward his ultimate goal. Numbers 5100 and 5111 were proof of that. The data was inconclusive but he was sure he was on the verge of a great discovery. Brooke would validate his newest breakthrough.

Some of the earlier mixed breeds had a changed amino acid that had caused a small change in the protein produced. This deficiency not only caused a rare brain disorder, but this disorder had been nearly undetectable. In addition, the earlier mixed breeds had a distinctive deformity—their left hand pinkie was angled rather than straight like the other nine fingers. Also, all the Ones had slightly larger eyes than the average human, not really noticeable unless you knew what to look for. He also had developed a new master gene that was accepted by the human body and had many applications he was currently working on.

Not that there had been many complaints. He simply wouldn't tolerate it. The humans were inferior, already unstable long before he showed up. The early tests on several humans resulted in mixed breeds that were psychotic in nature. These tests had actually furthered their cause as an indirect side effect, and thus, he had inadvertently furthered the cause. Of course, he claimed it had been his plan all along.

The genetic makeup of the different races had yielded varying final results that he had had to learn to circumvent. Many of these same individuals had been the catalysts for several wars and global disruptions due to their volatile and unstable natures. It had ultimately benefited the Ones.

Earlier, he had received a communique from Jonathon. Jonathon had told him that Victoria had escaped his capture. Fundor had apparently interfered again. Fundor, one of the originals Ones, had been asserting his superiority. Fundor was a fool. Jonathon, one of the first mixed breeds, was vastly more superior to him. Although those early years produced some highly unstable Ones, Jonathon had successfully survived and thrived.

Jonathon's first offspring, Jonathon, (he had named him Jonathon in his honor) had tried to kill him and had paid ultimately with his life. No one crossed Jonathon—no one. When he found out that he had actually sired two Ones, twins, and that the baby girl had, in fact, not died but had been quietly removed and hidden from his knowledge, he had begun a worldwide search to find her.

Chapter 22

They had received Intel from one of their info gatherers, as they called them. Dragone just called them spies. Sohayla had relayed the information he had been searching for. Her info had led them ultimately to Dr. Hardy's location. Bradley, the second spy, had just relayed significant Intel just within the last 24 hours. He had observed Brooke in a cell. He communicated she appeared to be unharmed. The teams were assembled quickly and plans were hastily, but cautiously, put into motion. They proceeded toward their target.

They gained access via the enhanced voice/iris mode detector. He used Dr. Hardy's level indicator. He signaled for his men to stop. Team One, headed by Matthew, a lethal, level-headed man who always got the job done, would be going in hard and fast. Team Two, headed by Dragone, would get the job done as well. Several of the men silently made their way in separate directions. Teams One's primary objective would be retrieval and annihilation, while

Team Two, the men and women with Dragone, would be in search and rescue mode.

Dragone moved with determination. They sought Brooke out. All indications were that she could be found somewhere on this floor. He would find Brooke and god help the bastards who took her. His quickly assembled team would retrieve Brooke and any information they could—then destroy what remained and who remained as well.

There was a lab technician approaching. He was moving down the hallway and he would intersect their locale within moments. He waited patiently until the startled tech looked at him. He struck with precision. His knife buried itself to the hilt. His heart impaled, he fell silently to the floor before he had a chance to scream.

Here, his men would avoid using the KOs because the surrounding energy would immediately alert the Ones to their presence. Not that he minded. He wanted to kill them all. Kill them for taking Brooke. Kill them for all their evil ways. He had known of their evilness long enough to know that they could easily take over the entire planet if the rebellion didn't gain the upper hand—and soon.

With the security system running a series of fake impressions, his team had only precious minutes before the system went down. They would then be besieged by countless Ones housed in the guard house within the compound. There were approximately twenty to twenty-five Ones there at any given time according to their Intel. And, there were many more dispersed throughout the compound.

Chapter 23

She decided thinking about other things were needed right now. Sitting on the cot, she let her thoughts drift away. Thinking back, it made no sense. Her parents had been killed in an auto related accident. It had been bothering her ever since Dragone had told her, her mom was killed because she was not healthy enough for the Ones' purposes.

Was their accident, not an accident after all? Why had the Ones played a part in their deaths? Were any of these people, here in this building, partly responsible? These Ones were pure evil, at least all the Ones she had met. Who was she really? According to Dragone, *she* was part Ones. Or was she? Feeling wholly human, she didn't think it possible she was anything else. She needed answers and it was driving her crazy.

She had been told by Dr. Hardy that she would be given the health assessment in a few short hours. The guard had told her she was to eat her food that had sat in the corner all morning long. She would not eat it.

Dr. Hardy walked into the room and asked Brooke why she hadn't eaten. Brooke walked over to the little table and picked up her food. She calmly returned to the cot and proceeded to throw her tray of food at Dr. Hardy's face. She had wanted to do much more to the little weasel, if she could have only gotten to him. The tray of scrambled eggs with something that looked like grits had worked though.

Waiting until he moved in close to the bars, she had took aim and flung them in his face. The eggs landed in his hair and face. The grits lay like a beige blanket over his once shiny black shoes. Brooke knew her temporary high at watching the egg stain on his lovely white lab coat and face were not going to last very long.

When he had recovered, he shook the bars in outraged anger. His eyes bulged as he said, "I'm going to kill you—slowly!"

Brooke took two steps back, wishing she could take back her egg and grit splatter assault. Her momentary pleasure was instantly replaced with fear.

He seemed to gather himself and calmed down. He looked at Brooke. His eyes bore into hers. She knew by the look in his eyes, he would do things to her that would be worse than anything she could possibly imagine. He would make the stories of

Stephen King seem like kindergarten fairy tales. *Please help me.*

"No, not kill you, not quite. Actually Brooke, I have something special planned just for you." He stood there looking at her saying nothing more. He turned and left the room.

Several of lab techs looked at her in stunned disbelief. With their mouths hanging open she turned and just looked downward. *I must find a way to get out of this hell hole. Think Brooke, think.*

Thinking was a mistake. She started to tremble just thinking about what he might have planned for her. She tried to brush the hair out of her eyes but her hands wouldn't work right. Her hands trembled, so much so, that she could only manage to push a few strands away. She just gave up and sat down—hard.

Chapter 24

The mess was cleaned up and no other food was offered. About an hour later a guard she had never seen approached. He unlocked the door and motioned for her to come out.

"I don't want to. I think I'll just stay here a while."

The guard responded, "I will carry you then." He started to extend his beefy hands toward her.

"Thanks, I've changed my mind. I'll follow you."

He pulled back his hand and waited. She walked forward only to be shoved along. They moved toward a door down the hall. He knocked.

"Enter," someone called from within.

The guard opened the door and grabbed Brooke's arm rather roughly and they moved together into the room. The interior was sterile and white. It had a lab set-up with gadgets and instruments everywhere. Several countertops had sterile-looking trays with scary looking implements presumably for surgery. Others had some type of high-tech gadgetry on them.

She didn't have too much time to take it all in because she heard soft, small sounds of distress. Like the whimpering of a dog when he desperately wants out. She looked in the direction the noises were coming from.

"Move it," said the guard.

She saw another door within the room and was shoved over to it. Having a bad feeling about this, she tried to slow her pace, but the guard only seemed to enjoy shoving her more.

This door had a glass window and what she briefly saw inside standing there made her stomach want to upheave anything she had left from the day before. Petrified, she refused to move. Her mind told her not to enter at all costs, that this was the room of nightmares, where all bad things happened, and then some.

Her mind must be playing tricks on her, she told herself. Being in magical realism most likely had that effect on you; because there was no possibility it could be real, could it?

The guard forced her to move into the room. It was quite large with a row of cages against the wall. There were things, or people—no, more like things, inside the cages. She wasn't really at all sure. Dr. Hardy was there staring at her in his surgical scrubs. He scared the shit out of her.

Her heart sank when she looked at the gurney. A patient was tied down on the gurney and the patient was fully awake. Although she was strapped down tightly, she was able to tilt her head to one side. She looked at Brooke with large, pleading eyes.

"Number 13602, this is a visiting guest. She will watch the proceedings so she might know what awaits her very soon."

Brooke stood there frozen in place, staring at the patient. She looked so helpless, so lost. Tears started to roll down the patient's cheeks as she turned away, resigned with the inevitable.

Dr. Hardy took a knife-like object and cut open a small portion of her mid-section. The patient screamed for several pitiful seconds before passing out. Dr. Hardy didn't seem to notice; he was so intent on his task. He moved several folds of skin and picked up something from a nearby tray and inserted it into the now unconscious patient.

She couldn't see what he had put in her and most definitely didn't want to know. He took his time and then stitched her up. Turning, he said to Brooke, "you will be here very soon and I will give you a surprise as well."

Just then, several of the creatures in the cages raddled the bars and wailed. The cages were metal, with bars across the front, and the remaining sides solid.

They reminded Brooke of the cages she had seen at the local ASPCA. The ASPCA had the kind of cages that housed dogs and cats that were looking for a home with a loving owner.

These cages, however, were of the human size. A row of four with four more stacked above. They were cast in shadows and she could only see what appeared to be people crouched in the back of the cages.

A few of them had had their backs to her, but now she could see the faces of a few. Man or woman, she couldn't tell, they all had malformations that her worst nightmares couldn't produce.

One creature looked as if he had body parts of a different species altogether. It had short fur on its face with one horn on the side. The other creature had red eyes that bore into her essence with its evil look. It wanted to be freed; with every intention to kill everyone in its path, for it was seized by a murderous rage. As it looked at her, it stuck out its paw through the bars and growled. She was numb.

"I see numbers 13510 and 13511 have woken up Brooke. Perhaps I will introduce you later. I have so many plans for you Brooke—so many plans." He started laughing. Like the mad scientist he was, he laughed in a way that it was most apparent insanity was a fine line that had already been crossed.

Brooke whispered, "He's mad." But the doctor had heard.

Turning, he said to Brooke, "Very astute of you. Some do say that, but never, ever, to my face. You have to be a little mad to be so brilliant, don't you think so?"

This couldn't be real. *Please, please, this can't be real. Let me wake up in my nice warm bed! Let me laugh away my fears.* In looking around, she saw only reality staring back at her. Biting her tongue to see if she could wake herself up, she only tasted the fear in her mouth. Her hands were shaking and sweat was breaking out. She brought the toe of her shoes together, touched her shirt, felt the texture and feel of it. It all felt real to her. She could smell the creatures; see their hideous, horrible, tortured faces.

The man was deranged and evil through and through. How could anyone do this? Why would anyone do this? It was all too much to grasp. Her brain was locked in a dizzying spiral of emotions. She was going to have a meltdown, right here, right now. Dread coursed through her like a living, breathing entity. It was as if the hands of evil were searching for her, and, she didn't know where to hide.

The stark realization that this was really happening brought about a new sense of urgency to escape. She started backing away from the scene of horrors but came up short when she bumped into the guard behind her. He roughly pushed her away and she fell to the floor.

As she was getting up, she looked over at the far wall and saw another creature that had turned to face her. This creature was a woman or at least mostly a woman. There were other, terrible things, growing out from her and she had a mad, wild look in her eyes. She looked over at Dr. Hardy and she yowled at him.

It was then that Brooke and the woman creature exchanged looks. The woman's eyes were pleading with her to help her. The sadness overwhelmed her sense of compassion. On some elemental level they cared for each other deeply. At that moment she would have given anything in the world to release her and ease her suffering. She mouthed, "I'm so sorry," silently to the woman. The woman just held her gaze.

"Get up now," said the guard and he kicked Brooke with the pointed edge of his hard-toed shoes. The woman hit the cage and roared. Brooke was hurting so badly she wanted to pass out, but was too afraid to. No, she mustn't. She stumbled forward and eventually got to her knees, slowly managing to stand. The pain was intense. He had kicked her in the lower part of the back; she found breathing difficult.

An orderly entered and took the patient on the gurney away down the hall. Brooke tried to catch her breath as Dr. Hardy systematically checked and rechecked the locks on each cage. There was some electronic system in place. She watched as the good doctor set the alarm for the cages pausing long enough to smile at the woman who had roared.

"You will pay for interrupting my work tonight, Bonita."

Bonita scooted back as far away from him as she was able, pushing herself up against the far end of the cage.

"That won't help you, Bonita. You should have behaved—too bad really."

Bonita began rocking back and forth in a clearly agitated state. He opened one of the nearby cages that had no one in it. He turned to Brooke, "you will be occupying this one in a few hours, but first we will have a little fun." He closed the cage and walked away, laughing at his own sick joke.

The guard started to advance on Brooke. "Move it bitch or I will have to show you who's in charge."

Still stunned, overwhelmed by what she had seen, and generally having a hard time processing it all, she quietly and cooperatively walked back. Back in her cell, she sat down on the cot and began formulating a plan. She did not want to end up like Bonita.

Chapter 25

As a child Brooke had always been good, really good with patterns. She had played mind games with Aunt Sissy and had a sneaky feeling Aunt Sissy had let her win on occasion.

She had memorized the sequence that Dr. Hardy had used to open the cage. He had not seemed concerned that she would see the sequence. It was a series of thirteen numbers. Most likely not easily memorized by most people—but Brooke was not like most people.

It was now late afternoon and many of the workers were going to leave for the day. Watching and waiting for just the right time, Brooke began to walk around the cell as if she was stretching a bit. The workers paid her no attention to her as they prepared to leave.

Not knowing if another night shift crew would be arriving, she decided to test her theory. She stepped over to where the front of her cell was, where the lock was, and gingerly looked around. No one was looking her way, and the guard was not in the room.

Her hand on the keypad, she put in the same sequence of numbers. It worked. The lock was disabled. She didn't move, didn't breathe. Screaming elation silently, she slowly walked over to the cot and sat down.

She concentrated on contacting Bonita. She felt in her mind the woman's thoughts, the rage she had inside, the confusion. Brooke didn't know how she knew these things. That had not happened with the animal in the forest.

Brooke explained to Bonita that she would try to help her, to free her; that she was to remain calm and do as she directed. She told her the sequence and demanded she try to reach the pad. She wasn't sure if it was possible or not. Her cage was not very far away. She got the impression that the other occupants were asleep and commanded Bonita not to let the others out.

As the last man exited the room she heard him say to the guard, "all is secure inside."

"Good," said the guard. "I need to hit the john."

She couldn't believe her good fortune. Waiting only long enough for the last worker to be well on his way, she stepped out of the cell and quickly made for the door. Brooke was out in the hallway and headed toward the creatures and Bonita. Fear was riding her hard now.

Footsteps… a guard was coming, probably just making his rounds. *Where do I hide?* Not sure where to go, she picked the closest door and tried the doorknob. It was locked. She moved on to the next closest door and again tried the lock. This time she found it was unlocked. She entered, did a quick evaluation, and quickly and quietly closed the door.

She was immersed in darkness. Total and absolute—like a breathing dragon waiting patiently for its prey to move before pouncing on it and devouring it. She stood frozen in place, listening for movement outside. Silently, she felt for the door handle and locked the door.

Ten seconds later someone tried the door and Brooke almost screamed. Almost, but she caught herself at the last possible moment. It had taken all her willpower not to react. It would have been easier if she had at least heard the approaching guard, right outside the door, but she hadn't.

One moment she was thinking about what to do, and in the next breath the doorknob and door were shaking violently. Not only did she almost scream, but she almost jumped backwards away from the door. The guard would have heard her for sure. He was just making his rounds she reminded herself. She tried to calm down, talk to herself, but her heart was racing and she couldn't seem to breathe.

She was on edge. Who wouldn't be? She knew what was waiting for her if they found her. She would rather die. Dying would be much more pleasant than what they had planned for her, no doubt about it.

She waited until she could hear the receding footsteps move down the hall, and still she waited. With no noises she could detect, she decided to chance turning on a light. With a small click the lights turned on. She looked around for what she hoped would be a weapon she could take with her. No such luck. Only papers and files in this room.

She started to leave when she got that funny feeling, like an impression in her mind, giving her guidance. She was not about to look a gift horse in the mouth. She went over to the small desk—began to look around. Although dusty and dirty it had a laptop sitting on top. It was an IBM ThinkPad.

In a desk drawer she found pens and pencils. In the second drawer she tried she spotted a USB stick 64 giga-byte and plugged it in. She uploaded all the files she could fit. She shoved it in her pants pocket and moved toward the door.

A shipping label on top of the stacked boxes next to the door caught her attention and she grabbed it too. It went in her pants pocket as well.

Cautiously peeking out from the door she glanced in both directions. Seeing no one and not hearing anyone approaching, she took a tentative step forward. She hoped she was going in the right direction. Moving as quietly and as swiftly as she dared, she made her way to the door where nightmares resided within.

She opened the door. The lights came on automatically so Brooke knew she had to hurry. Bonita was already out of the cage looking around, pacing, as if she didn't know what to do. She approached Bonita and offered her hand. Bonita took it and started to cry. Pulling Bonita toward the door Brooke had almost made it to the hallway when Bonita dug in her heels, stopped, and screamed.

"Shh…, please understand. We must leave. We *must* leave," said Brooke imploring her to understand. Bonita yanked her hand free, causing Brooke to stumble, and ran back to the alarm.

"No Bonita no!" Brooke got up and ran to Bonita praying she wouldn't do it. As if in slow motion, she saw Bonita punch the last number in and the cages all opened. Brooke barely had time to react and make a mad dash for the door, before the hideous creature that had growled at her jumped down and ran for the door.

Brooke somehow made it to the outside of the first door. She held the door knob closed from the other side but knew the strength of the creature would soon force her to let go. He was incredibly strong and he was pulling on the door with all his might. She couldn't see Bonita but she could hear several different screams from within. Looking around she saw the tray of instruments still on the countertop not more than 10 to 12 feet away. Perhaps she could use it to defend herself. *If,* she could make it to the tray before the creature got to her, that is.

She heard approaching footsteps coming down the hall. She quickly looked back over her shoulder as the guard appeared.

"Bitch, this time… What the hell? …" He never finished his question.

Brooke let the door go and moved to the far left. The guard didn't even have time to lift his gun up. The creature was on him in an instant. Ripping and clawing his chest open. Blood was literally flying in all directions.

She wasted no time running past the creature. Before she could get out of the door, blood splattered on the side of her face and clothes.

Brooke ran for her life down the long hallway and through a sliding double door. There were two guards sitting at the station. They jumped up when they saw Brooke, but she didn't care. She dived behind the guards, as the creature was right behind her. She ran past them to a set of doors that looked like it led to the outside compound. Screams of agony filled her head as she tore through the doors.

It was just a small outside area that led to the next building. Although there was a small patch of grass and bushes on both sides along with two wooden benches, the ten foot brick wall prevented her from gaining access to the outside world.

Seeing no other option, she opened the next set of double doors and entered. Looking for a place to hide and seeing none, she continued running at full speed down the hallway.

She paused long enough to test a couple doors. They were firmly locked. She heard the doors open and close. Someone was coming. The creature had entered the building. *At least I'll die quick*, thought Brooke.

She picked up speed as she rounded a corner and ran smack into Dragone. Although she fell backwards, his rock hard body had stayed stationary. He was already moving in front of her toward the newest threat he could hear coming down the hallway like a freight train.

"Behind me! Behind me, Dragone," is all she had time to say before he pushed her down and drew his weapon. He stepped into the corridor and pointed it toward the creature. As it ran straight for him, he shot the creature once in between the eyes. It fell hard to the floor, dead.

Dragone reached down and helped Brooke to her feet. He saw that she had blood plastered all over her face and clothes. "Brooke, are you hurt?" His hands started exploring.

"No, no. I'm fine. I'm so much better now." As she stood up she grabbed his shirt with both hands, pulled him close. She buried her head in his shirt. She inhaled his scent, earthly and wonderful. He was hesitant for only a moment, but then put his arms around her and held on.

He softly said into her ear, "Brooke, we must move quickly."

"No, we can't leave yet."

"Brooke, I know you're probably in shock; I can only imagine. But we must leave. Forget anything you left back there, honey."

Brooke grabbed his arms tight. "No, you don't understand, Bonita is back there. I left her in that hellhole." Moving away from his embrace she turned to head back.

She looked down and immediately moved to the far right up against the wall. She did not want to look at the body of the creature. Even though it had wanted to kill her, she could not find it in her to judge it. What the "good" doctor had done to it, she couldn't fathom. She felt such sorrow for it, and was glad he was now at peace.

"Who's Bonita?" Dragone said as he and his men followed Brooke back down the hall. "We only have a few minutes before all hell is going to break loose Brooke."

"I have to know. I have to know if she's alive. We have to help her. Please Dragone."

"Okay, okay. How far down the hall is it?"

"Not far."

They walked back through the corridor and saw the manacled bodies of the two guards that the creature had viciously ripped apart. Brooke tried not to look but she saw pieces of internal organs lying to the side of one body, an arm of another. The dark blood was pooled around the dead.

Moving faster now, they passed the bodies. They went down the hallway with no interference. They came to the room that had housed the experiments.

Dragone led the way in. The smell assailed their nostrils and gagged their throats. The walls had been sprayed with blood. What remained of the guard was now indistinguishable. He looked like a huge clump of body tissue with very little blood actually pooled on the floor. Most of the guard's blood seemed to be on the walls. It was hideous. Even these hardened men, some of whom had been to the farthest corners of the world, had experienced the stench of death, the sights and sounds of war, found it hard to look at, to imagine how painful these wounds must have been before the moment of death.

They moved on, to the next interior room. The sound of whimpering could be heard. Several things, creatures, people, whatever they had been or were now lay about the room dead or dying. That is, all but one. Bonita was huddled in the corner quivering. Brooke pushed past Dragone and knelt beside her. Other than an open wound on her arm that was now just slightly bleeding, she looked to be okay. She put her arm around Bonita's shoulder.

"Bonita, I need you to come with us. I will help you. Everything will be alright."

Bonita looked up at Brooke nodding her head, acknowledging she understood.

The men, including Dragone, couldn't help but look at Bonita before they left the room. She had obvious growths on her that made her look like a science fiction experiment from the dark side. But the men were all business as they approached the door.

"Brooke, listen to me. Bonita and you need to stay behind us at all times. If I give you an instruction, I need to you follow it without any hesitation, okay?"

"Yes, I understand. I'll follow without any hesitation Dragone, I promise."

With that out of the way, he led the small group out into the hall. They went back the way they had come. An alarm sounded. Before they had reached the first set of double doors soldiers poured into the hallway. The men went in low and blasted several guards. But there were plenty more where they had come from.

Dragone screamed, "Fall back, fall back." The men along with Brooke and Bonita moved backwards down the hall. Their options were few. One of Dragone's men fell from a bullet wound to his head. He was dead. They continued to fight while retreating backwards looking for somewhere to go. Brooke turned and saw a fire alarm with a fire hose in a separate box. She broke the glass with the attached rod and turned it on. Spraying the approaching Ones gave the team enough time to regroup. They used their KOs on the Ones one by one until the remaining Ones retreated.

Dragone motioned for the team to move out the door to the compound grounds. Within two minutes a helicopter appeared; it touched down but not before it had used its firepower to ensure a safe landing. All the soldiers held their positions until Brooke and Bonita were aboard, and then they climbed on as well.

One of the soldiers turned to Dragone. "Sir, Team One has placed all devices, sir."

"Thank you, Armando."

Team One had their orders and would carry out their mission with precision.

"How are you Brooke?"

He looked like he wanted to say much more but knew it was neither the time nor place. It would wait.

She looked up into his eyes. His eyes said a lot. She had intended to hold all her bottled up fears, elation at being rescued, and her state of total confusion, until she was alone and could let it all out. But his eyes provoked the flood gates open, even though she tried in vain to hold it back.

No longer caring for those around her, she buried her head on Dragone's chest. Her feelings were overwrought, too raw, and too close to the surface. It started as a quiet sob that quickly turned into much more. It was a kind of mournful wail that told you the depths of her despair.

The men kept their faces straight ahead with a blank expression but it was impossible not to feel the pain, not to be moved by the soft, anguished, aching of her heart.

So much pain and suffering, and for what? Money, power, greed—what? Brooke could not understand the mentality of people like those she had just left. How, just how, could trivial things like money guide your every move? Surely, they knew they couldn't carry anything with them into the afterlife. Without people like Dragone, these monsters, would rule over all, she mused.

She cried softly, with a terrible, agonizing, sorrowful tone. Time was lost to her until Bonita put her hand on her leg and lightly squeezed, to let her know she was there for her. Somehow that reached her brain. Ending her bout of melancholy, Brooke turned to Bonita with a tear-stained face.

She studied Bonita's face, finding it beautiful. Dr. Hardy had done unspeakable acts to Bonita, but he could not take her true beauty away. Sniffing, she hugged Bonita, no words were necessary. She was wearing her heart on her sleeve.

Chapter 26

They arrived in the dead of the night. As she emerged from the helicopter, she saw barbed wire on the fence posts not far away. There were men and women in uniform with guns at their sides.

They approached a hillside that appeared barren. Nonetheless, Dragone directed her to stand by the mound of dirt and wait. "Why are we doing this?"

"You'll see," said Dragone.

A door opened where moments before there was nothing more than a patch of grass and weeds. Brooke was led into a building. Bonita immediately grabbed her hand, fearful they would be separated. Brooke held her hand, and put her arm entwined through hers, for reassurance. Lights came on within. She looked over to Dragone with utter amazement. She said, "Who are you?" He simply smiled and entered. The door closed quickly behind them.

They walked down a long hallway. Brooke was feeling uneasy about, what, exactly, would happen now. Bonita seemed as nervous as Brooke. Bonita was visibly agitated; she started mumbling to herself, further concerning Brooke.

They were met by several men and women who were waiting for them. After talking with Bonita, several team members took them to a room where Bonita could refresh and relax. It took some coaxing, though. They were ushered into a small room where two women were waiting. They explained to Brooke and Bonita they were there to help. They told Bonita this room would provide a safe haven for much needed rest and recuperating. Later a doctor would visit with her.

The women would stay with her around the clock from this point forward unless she requested otherwise. Both women, Brooke and Bonita, were given assurances that they would see each other often each day. Brooke talked it over with Bonita and left the decision to leave the room up to her.

Whispering Bonita said, "Do you trust these people?

"I do. I really believe they have our best interests at heart. They will take good care of you. I promise to see later. I will be there for you every step of the way. Don't worry."

Speaking softly Bonita said, "Okay. I will see you later, right? Please…, you will be back here soon won't you?" Bonita's body language demonstrated that she was feeling very nervous. Bonita was wringing her hands over and over; she just couldn't stop herself and she had her legs crossed. She shook her leg in clear agitation.

Bonita liked these people but she couldn't be sure. She doubted if she could ever be sure about anything ever again. Bonita liked Brooke, and she wanted to believe what Brooke said to be true, but she couldn't be sure. Things were jumbled up in her mind. Bonita knew people stared at her when they thought she wasn't aware, but she was aware that they stared, that they thought she was a freak. Bonita used to stare at freaks and feel sorry for them. Now she was a freak and a half.

"Yes, I promise."

Bonita looked at Brooke trying to decide. Brooke didn't move, just stood there waiting. Bonita took her time thinking things through; although her thoughts these days were sketchy at best, she shook her head in acceptance.

Brooke walked away after having hugged Bonita tightly for several minutes. She was told someone was waiting to see her. Dragone had discreetly waited for her in the hallway. He walked with her saying nothing. After walking several steps, he offered his hand. Brooke was so touched she started to silently cry. The offer of his hand in that moment had mattered. She took hold of his strength and held on.

Incredibly tired, both physically and mentally, she walked down the hall wishing she could just leave this place. Fly like a bird to a branch high above the noise, the people, and pain. She would eat worms and live a simple life. No Ones hunting for her. No labs or mad scientists waiting for her blood. She just wanted a rest. A rest from all this insanity, was that too much to ask? She screamed silently to the heavens above, wanting some sign. Some sign that she could use as guidance moving forward. Some small sign that would tell her why this was happening and why it was so important she be a part of it.

Why couldn't someone else take her place and fight the Ones. She was just an antique store owner, owner of the, "Again in the Spotlight" store. Probably these people, this so called rebellion, were comprised of men and women that were highly trained professionals in this sort of thing. What did she know?

Soldiers went to boot camps somewhere she had never seen. Soldiers went to foreign lands and fought wars she never had to witness. She supported many worthy causes that she never had to participate in. In short, in the past, she cared deeply about the plight of others, only she looked at things from afar never up close and personal. There were too many thoughts swirling around in that brain of hers and she needed a respite from all the stress.

Victoria was waiting for her in the front hall. They embraced each other and said nothing; they both were crying. Brooke had wanted, no, needed to see Claire, Victoria, whomever, so badly. Right now, her emotions were swapping her. They just needed to touch each other, embrace each other, so that she might know she was in the real world and not a dream world. Slowly she stepped back, "Are you real, Claire?"

"Yes Brooke, I'm really here."

"God, I've missed you. I have so many questions."

"I will try to answer them all. Let me introduce you to my husband, Trevor. Trevor, this is my cousin, Brooke."

"Nice to finally meet you Brooke," said Trevor.

"Husband?" She looked over to Victoria with a questioning stare. Turning back to Trevor she said, "Nice to meet you too."

From out of the clear blue, and with just a moment's notice, she was practically mowed down by 60 pounds of fur. Sammy was there jumping and kissing Brooke.

"Down, Sammy. Down," demanded Victoria.

"He's fine Claire, Victoria, whoever." She bent over and hugged him. He was so happy to see her again. Brooke was equally happy. She had been worried about what might have happened to him. While petting him Brooke noticed Dragone was looking intently at her.

Dragone had known it would end like this, he just didn't think it would be so hard. He started to back away. He was going to miss Brooke, but it was better this way, he told himself. He didn't try to decipher why he felt this way. Brooke made him feel things he long ago had put away in a box and had thrown into the farthest corners of his mind. He knew he was lying to himself. He knew she was special.

He needed to get back to slaying the Ones. That was the only thing he was really good at. She was an innocent. Already the things that happened so far were terrible for her. He had let those things happen to her. He was solely to blame. By all rights she should hate him.

Looking up, she saw Dragone backing away. "Dragone, where are you going?" questioned Brooke.

"I need to get back to work. I'm sure you have a lot of catching up to do. Nice to see you again, Victoria, Trevor." They nodded in turn smiling at Dragone. He returned the nod then turned and walked away without looking back.

Still loving on Sammy, Brooke had both her arms around his head. Victoria said, "You should see him with Sunny. It's hilarious."

"Who's Sunny?" asked Brooke.

"Sunny is my lovable, naughty cat. Sammy and Sunny love each other. Sunny likes to stalk Sammy and pounces when he least expects it. You have to see it to believe it."

"I can't wait. I've missed you." Brooke couldn't help it, her eyes starting misting over. If she didn't stop now she was going to embarrass herself, again. She felt overwhelmed with conflicting emotions. Elated that she was with her cousin, but uncertain what to do about Dragone; she wanted to just go somewhere quiet and figure things out.

"I have missed you as well. We have so much to talk about."

Trevor said, "I will leave you ladies until later. I'm sure you wish to catch up on a great deal of things." He leaned over and kissed Victoria. He took his time and savored it, whispered sweet nothings in her ear.

Trevor always made Victoria smile. "See you later handsome."

Brooke and Victoria walked down the hallway toward a quiet room with Sammy following behind. The hallway led to a separate wing with wide double doors. The hallway held pieces of art in various modes. There was a sculpture sitting in a recessed alcove below a skylight that enhanced the overall effect. Further down the hallway, there was a print or perhaps an original Monet hanging on the wall.

They sat down and just hugged each other again. After a few minutes, Brooke spoke up. "Tell me how, in the course of just two short weeks, my life has been turned not only upside down, but inside out as well. I don't ever remember being this scared. Not even when we snuck downstairs and watched *The Shining* from behind the stair railings when I was eleven years old. I didn't sleep for a week because I was terrified someone was coming for me."

Victoria laughed at the memory of watching *The Shining* with Brooke. Aunt Sissy had lectured her for watching it and for allowing Brooke to see it as well. Her library privileges had been taken away for a week. Aunt Sissy had known what Victoria cared most about.

Victoria talked about the Ones and their agenda. She told Brooke about what she had discovered about herself. Victoria, known as Claire to her family, was a chosen one. She explained that she was the grand-daughter of a set of twins that just so happened to be part Ones. Additionally, Victoria's grandmother had been separated at birth, believed to be dead, and raised by members of the rebellion in an attempt to keep her safe. On her death bed, she had revealed the truth, which had led to someone betraying her trust, and thus the hunt for Victoria had begun. Luckily, Trevor had been picked to be her protector. Trevor was apparently perfect for the job in more ways than one.

Since discovering her true identity, she had visited the Forgotten Caves and had acquired a vast amount of knowledge from those who came before her. She now led the rebellion along with Trevor.

Brooke said, "By the way, I almost forgot, I have this shipping label and order summary, along with some other things I retrieved from the compound. She took out the papers and the USB thumb drive.

Brooke's head was ready to implode in on itself. She told Victoria she needed to get some sleep. Real sleep without any interruptions and a hot bath. Clean clothes would be nice as well. Victoria smiled and told her all the preparations had been taken care of. They decided to hold off on any more explanations until tomorrow.

Much later, in her own separate quarters, she sat in the lounge chair and thought about Dragone. How, in just a very short time, he had become the focal point of all her thoughts. Something was nagging her. Something Dragone had said about his grandparents being killed. She couldn't quite put her finger on it but there was something, something she was missing, something that didn't quite sit right with her. Along with her newfound ability with animals, Brooke had always had a bit of heightened intuition. There was no rhyme or reason to it. Sometimes she intuitively knew stuff and sometimes she didn't.

Dragone had told her that his grandparents were killed in a car accident and that he didn't have any other siblings. That had been a lie. There were other siblings, she was sure of it. Why that mattered at all, she wasn't sure. But, somehow she knew that there was a connection with the Ones.

She needed to ask him about what happened, specifically, and then she would tell him what she knew to be true. Her intuition told her it was important, very important.

Right now it was very important, paramount even, that she figure out a way to make Dragone realize that they were destined to be together. That together they would make a difference.

Chapter 27

It was a beautiful day in spring. Many of the trees, bushes, and flowers had started to blossom. And allergy season was upon them all. Several of the members of the rebellion were suffering along with Brooke. As they travelled downtown they passed a handful of maintenance workers cutting the grass in the median, adding to their misery. She quickly rolled up the window of the Hummer and sneezed off and on all the way back to the compound.

Thinking back, over her lifetime up till now, she realized how special and wonderful her life had been. She knew she had had many good friends, men and women, who really cared about her in her life as an antique owner. She would miss them terribly. She hoped to see them occasionally, but realistically knew that might just be wishful thinking.

It had been two months since she had last seen Dragone. She had been very busy with the sale of her store. It had been heart wrenching but necessary.

The new owner had loved her store since the day it had opened.

Rebecca Hanover, Becky to her friends, had promised to keep the essence of her vision alive. She would continue to hunt out the best finds and sell them at a fair and profitable price. Her loyal customer base would continue to shop there.

Coming to terms with the sale had been exceedingly difficult at first, but she had resided herself to the inevitable. She knew she had to seek protection in numbers. Ashley would be working there for as long as she wanted. Becky had even gone, so far as, to offer Ashley a future position finding and buying antiques. Something Ashley had been thoroughly excited about. As Becky was now in her 60's, she anticipated the need for less travel soon.

Closer to the home front, Bonita had undergone three surgeries since arriving at the compound. The transformation was remarkable. Bonita was still in therapy, probably would be for a very long time, but she was slowly returning to Bonita, a bright, funny, lovable person that had much more living to do. They would be friends forever.

Dr. Hardy, however, had effectively disappeared without a trace. He was seen by one of the team members escaping just before they blew up the compound. Local news reports had indicated that the local fertilizer plant had self-ignited causing extensive damage.

Hoping Dr. Hardy would never reappear, she thought about what he would have likely done to her if she had not escaped. It was a chilling thought. He was everything that the word evil embodied. Never having hated or wished someone any misfortune before, it felt uncomfortable. Dr. Hardy had a rotten, putrid, decayed mind. He deserved the most severe punishment possible. Actually, the guard deserved it too. All the Ones needed it, the whole damn lot.

She had been brought up to speed on the Ones. It was unbelievable. Almost beyond her comprehension, really inconceivable; they fit right in and no one knew. She probably stood in line behind an Ones in the grocery store. Maybe she sat in class with one, or even tutored one. A more horrible thought, maybe one of those disaster dates she'd had in college had been with one.

She reminded herself, she had the Ones blood running in her, as well. The difference was, she was not an Ones. She loved, cared, and contributed to her community and country—that mattered. It would be a tragedy to let these Ones destroy their world and take over.

We, the people, had fought, suffered, bled, and survived. We, for the most part, loved our land, honored ourselves, and our neighbors. Although there were most definitely some people among us that were truly evil, there was a justice system in place that held us together. Not a perfect system for sure, but the best that we have. These abominations didn't care about this land and all the inhabitants therein. They were just users, needing us to further their cause, and they would most certainly destroy this world.

She had come to a major decision, one that would hopefully change her life and those around her—for all time. She would not let Dragone go. She couldn't. She knew he was the man for her and she was sure he felt the same. She just needed to convince him a little. She had asked around and Dragone was in his rooms in Building 100. He was due to leave in three days' time. It would have to be enough. She went back to her room to devise a foolproof plan. Their future happiness was on the line.

Brooke tended to think that each decision, big and small, had insignificant to better than a slightly small impact on the people around her. It was a gross error that she fooled herself with. From the person she let in front of her at the checkout counter, because he only had two items; to the lady she wouldn't let deliberately butt in front of her at the movie ticket line.

The man she let go in front of her at the checkout counter may have had enough time to make a hasty phone call to his fiancé to say he was sorry about their argument, only to discover her lover answered the phone. Or perhaps, the man had time to just barely catch a cab that turned out to be driven by a cabbie, Peter, who suggests he buy a Powerball ticket because the drawing was in a couple of hours. He consequently ends up winning millions in the drawing.

The lady who she refused to allow to butt in front of her, had to go to the end of the line, and, therefore, didn't have time to quickly cross the street to grab a snow cone to enjoy while waiting, so she didn't get hit by the speeding car that ran the red light. Or, maybe by being forced to the end of the line, she gets mad and leaves only to be mugged and beaten by a gang while on her way home.

We all are interconnected with each other. No matter how much we thought we led a solitary life outside of our immediate family, the truth was life was unpredictable, happy, sad, and wonderful; everything she wanted and so much more. It dawned on her that she wouldn't be able to appreciate all the good, truly appreciate, without the bad. Maybe 'the bad' were some kind of cosmic balance in the universe.

This experience had changed her. So many things seemed different now. The sky seemed more beautiful; she even liked to look at the low flying airplanes in the air space near the airport. The car in front of her that needed a muffler repair didn't bother her. Standing in line wasn't going to deter her. Her sighs had become routine. Now, however, the little things were just that, little.

Her life could have been over several times by now. Each moment, each smile, each hug, each sunset, was the most precious of all now. She didn't want to lose or waste a minute of it. There was a whole lot of life out there.

She went over to the windows, pulled back one sheer drape. The wood floors had dark cherry shading that accentuated the Persian rugs that laid over them. She ran her feet gently over the floor, feeling the smooth texture. The coolness soothed her tired feet. The walls were a hint of gray with white molding along with crown molding throughout. The ceilings were at least 12 feet high with a tray ceiling that made the room seem larger than it actually was.

There were three dressers that had marble tops with inlay intricate details throughout. Touching the marble, she let her fingers move over the dresser to feel the richness, the quality craftsmanship. She moved on to the oversized arm chair and ottoman that were simple in a brocade design. Everything in this room was specifically put there by a very talented person. No detail was left out. The room was simply exquisite.

She was sure Jacqueline would love this place. Walking back over to the bank of windows on the far side of the room, she pushed the white sheer drapes gently to the side. Gazing out the window, she thought about how much things had changed for her. She thought about all the things she wanted to happen now in her life.

She would not weigh on the past; she wanted the future to include Dragone, and that must be her focus now. Three days, she had only three days. He could be going anywhere, gone for a long time, perhaps months. A need formed in her mind and grew until it was almost an obsession. Knowing this was something bigger than just Dragone and herself, she let her thoughts wander and explore.

Although chilly, it was a gorgeous night. Opening the French doors, she stepped out onto the stone balcony. Wrapping her arms around her chest in an effort to warm herself, she gazed out into the darkness.

Growing up, the dark was a distant scary place, that as a kid she remembered stories her classmates told of the boogieman that was waiting for you. Most monster movies she could remember seeing, usually had a bad guy or monster that hid in the dark. They didn't seem to bother you during the daylight hours—no—just during the darkness. But, here, tonight, darkness held a special kind of beauty and it seemed more beautiful than scary.

Black was Brooke's favorite color. It looked good on her, aiding in her ability to appear slimmer and it pleased her when she looked in the mirror. Black held an allure that no other color seemed to emit. Black, she mused, was a combination of all the different colors put together, so it must be special, perhaps even spiritual.

You could see thousands of stars above tonight. The moon shone so bright that some of the surrounding stars close to the moon just faded away. As she looked up, a shooting star passed by the heavens above that left her in awe. An impression of the streak stayed in her vision for a few seconds more.

She had only witnessed one other shooting star before. That had been on a camping trip with her family many years before. They had driven by car out west to Montana with a tent and a map, only to have the best time of their lives.

The groupings of stars were a sight to see. In the city, most clear nights the most you could hope for was a few stars here and there to look upon. Here, where the night sky was not encumbered by the hordes of artificial lights that interfered with the real light show above. Here, your sight was only hindered by your own limitations.

Where out there did the Ones come from? Was their planet like Earth's? She pondered, as she looked up and out to where the galaxies resided. What would this new reality mean for the future of humans? She would move forward; there really was only one option she could see; she would embrace and make the most of it.

Her hands, in an effort to warm her, swiftly rubbed her arms up and down. Being honest with herself, she knew her heart recognized and needed Dragone. It was something that couldn't be rationally explained. In this lifetime, right now, at this point in time, she needed him with every fiber of her existence. She would not let uncertainty hold her back. Even with all the upheaval her family was experiencing, all the unknowns, she would find a way. The glass was half full, not half empty. It was all good.

She left her rooms and proceeded to walk to Dragone's building before she could talk herself out of it. The unknown was what was slowing her down, trying to stop her. What if he had only meant it to be a one-night stand? What if he had, in fact, moved on? Maybe he hadn't felt the same as she. So many questions, with only one way to know the answer to, she continued to move forward.

There was no Plan B; if he rejected her she would be devastated. She would not beg though. She would respect his decision. She owed him that much.

Before she knew it, she was at his door. Now or never, she took a deep breath to steady herself. Terror, just as real as any she had ever felt, was in her hip pocket. *I can do this.* She knocked on the door. It took a few seconds but he answered the knock.

"Brooke. Is something wrong?" He gestured for her to come in. "Come in." His eyes took her all in and soaked up her essence.

"No, nothing is wrong and everything is right."

She entered his room and glanced around. It was lavishly furnished like her room, but with more masculine tones. Bold reds and browns, with accents of orange, she would never have picked that combination, but somehow it worked here grouped together. She guessed that was why Jacqueline was the interior designer and not her.

Now that she was here, her shyness or nerves, were kicking in, being afraid to ask the question, for fear of the answer she might just receive.

"I wanted to speak with you in person."

"Of course, Brooke, sit down please."

He forced himself not to go to her, but he wanted her badly. Keeping his face non-emotional as possible, he didn't want to give away his true feelings. It was better this way. Staying away from her been had one of the hardest things he had ever had to do. His friend, Tony, had kept him informed. Selling her store and moving into the compound here must have been hard on her.

He didn't know if he would be able to keep his promise being this close to Brooke. He'd promised himself to stay away, permanently. She deserved more than he had to offer. Not only was he difficult to be with; his life was what you would call, complicated. He hunted and killed Ones, moved around a lot, didn't have much money or much of anything to offer Brooke. He couldn't further complicate her life by asking her to be with him.

"How have you been?"

"Fine."

Okay. Now what? She wanted to blurt out that she loved him. That she yearned for him every day they were apart. That the nights were the worst—lying in bed night after night, wanting him, needing him; imagining his arms around her, holding her close, making love to her until the morning sun rose high in the sky.

Instead of telling him things she found too hard to put to words, she said, "Where did your travels take you this time?"

"I was assigned to intercept a courier at Los Alamos. He was delivering sensitive information."

"I see." This was getting her nowhere.

"Are you going to be staying here at the compound for a while?"

"No, I plan to ask to be assigned to a new mission right away." *So I can be so far from you, I'm not tempted.*

So, it's true. He doesn't want me. She had fabricated the whole scenario in her mind. He probably had someone else. And, why wouldn't he? She had been nothing but trouble for him since the beginning. Being obliged to save her time and again, traipsing after her through the forest, having to go on a rescue mission into that dreadful compound, and the thought about all the good people that had been hurt as a result of her stupidity, it was no wonder he no longer wanted anything to do with her. He probably thought she was wanton, the way she had acted, practically throwing herself at him. *I need to save what little pride I have left, and leave.*

The hurt was building inside, churning and twisting, until it would open old wounds, create a hole so deep, so wide, her soul would be swallowed up, leaving her incomplete and incapable of ever loving again. Her eyes showed nothing, her body language numb. This blow would leave her dead inside.

"Brooke?"

"Yes."

"Are you listening? I asked you a question."

"Sorry, I'm not a very good guest. I need to get going." She got up and headed for the door. Crying in front of him would be the ultimate humiliation. She just couldn't do it here, she had to get away.

"Don't be sorry. I'm the one who is sorry. I put you through a lot. I'm surprised you came here to talk to me. You have every right to hate me."

Those words made her stop and turn around. "What are you saying? I behaved like a spoiled brat, at the cost of many people being hurt, all because of me. I know what you must think of me. It was a mistake to come here. I had hoped you could forgive me."

Too upset, nearing the edge of her control, she said, "I need to leave now, before I make a bigger fool of myself."

He grabbed her then. She turned into his waiting arms, hugged him tight, never wanting to let go. He embraced her body as he knew he couldn't resist. He wanted her, he wanted her.

Not caring, he ravished her mouth; he took in her essence, so hungry for her these last months. He thought that being apart so long he would adjust and things would return to normal, fighting and killing Ones. He had been wrong. He ached every waking moment for her, yearned for her. He could not forget how soft she seemed for him. How she fit; conformed to his body, perfect in every way. His sleep was evaded by haunting memories of her touch, her feel, her smell. Now he knew that he needed Brooke much like animals needed water to drink. So he drank.

As he kissed her, she was lost in an ecstasy so sweet, there was no adequate comparison she could label it by in heaven or earth. No one could compare to this man. His uniqueness was made for her. They complimented each other in ways she could never have fathomed.

"Brooke, I have missed you. Do you want this as much as I?"

"Yes, yes Dragone, absolutely, yes."

He swept her into his arms, never letting go of her lips, and carried her into his bedroom. He gently laid her down on top of the comforter and took off first her top and then her bra. Hands everywhere, touching, feeling, absorbing all that she was, he couldn't have enough of her. Time went by without a care.

She was lost in forever land, and she never wanted to leave. His world was full of exquisite feelings, the kind that left you breathless and wanting more and more until there was a fine line between pleasure and pain. His hands were gentle and thorough, finding every point on her skin to bring her that much closer, higher she flew like a soaring eagle to a pinnacle on the mountaintop. Time stood still.

Minutes or perhaps hours later, Brooke had no idea; she stirred in Dragone's arms. They had solidly bonded. Definitely not just sex, they had shared an experience unlike anything anyone could possibly have and still be grounded here on Earth. She had entrusted her heart and soul into Dragone's safe keeping. Smiling, she turned to face Dragone. She lovingly touched his face, memorizing every aspect of his face. The contour, the planes and angles, the coloring and highlights of his hair, it was all beautiful to her. "I love you."

Dragone seemed taken aback, but quickly recovered, smiled. "I love you."

Chapter 28

Xen awaited the decision from the Supreme Leader. Although not engaged in the battle that was taking place, his proximity to the location would alert the Ones to his position. He wanted them to know. They were vermin of the lowest order. He awaited their fate and that of the mixed breeds.

Word came from the Supreme Leader of his kind, Mintaka. Xen was given his directives. It would be done at the moon's next rising.

Please enjoy an excerpt from
my upcoming book,

Hope And Destiny

(The Darkest Series)

Bret had asked Jacqueline to meet him at the Tiki Tiki Lounge on Franklin Boulevard. It was a popular hangout. She thought this would be as good a place as any to tell him. Bret and Jacqueline had had a falling out these last couple of weeks. They felt passionately different about a whole range of ideas, which caused considerable discussion and exhausting debates. She just couldn't see the point in remaining in this relationship anymore.

As she sat down at the table he had reserved, she saw several couples and what appeared to be several single people mingling as well. She didn't know why he had asked her to meet him here tonight, but she thought that maybe he was feeling the same way about their relationship as she did. They had dated for three months now and it just wasn't working out between them.

Jacqueline had just finished telling Bret she thought they should end things now while they were still on speaking terms, when a shout went up that it was someone named Amy's birthday today.

"Just a second, I can't hear you," Bret gestured with his finger to his ear. A small group of waiters and waitresses sang Happy Birthday to the young woman sitting a few tables away. It ended with a lot of clapping and cheering.

A few minutes later as the noise died down, they were able to carry on a normal conversation once again. "As I was saying, Bret, we can remain friends and I would be happy to help you out when you move into that new apartment on the 15th."

"Thanks, Jacqueline. I think we're making the right choice here." Bret seemed relieved with the decision as well.

They discussed things with civility and each wished the other the very best. They promised to stay in touch as much as possible. At least there wasn't going to be any unpleasantness like Jacqueline's friend Reece had experienced recently.

Just last week, Reece and Jacqueline had met up at the local book club monthly meeting. Afterwards, they went to a little Mexican restaurant nearby. Reece told her how her former boyfriend, Todd, took the news that she didn't want to date any longer. She went on to explain that she had tried to make Todd understand she felt the need to end things between them; that things were becoming uncomfortable to the point that Reece felt compelled to end it; and that things would be better this way.

Todd had not taken the news well. He had upturned his plate on the table and stormed out, leaving Reece having to apologize and pay the bill.

She later found out he had went on social media and had spread detailed private information about her life.

These days you had to be really careful about sharing information with your partner. It was a slippery slope. If you held all your personal information back, then your partner would assume you were not ready to commit. If you shared your most intimate family details, and every family had one or two embarrassing secrets, then you could potentially end up getting burned like Reece.

Jacqueline was very pleased Bret was taking the breakup in stride. Perhaps he had felt the same, and wanted to move on. Thinking back, Bret hadn't shared that much personal information with her. Yes, this would be for the best. Her needs were not being met with Bret—time to move on.

Jacqueline and Bret split the bill. Back out on the street Jacqueline kissed Bret's cheek and said goodbye. Bret, always being the gentlemen, insisted on walking Jacqueline to her car. He said "you just never know when or where something bad might happen."

Jacqueline rolled her eyes, but nonetheless accepted his offer.

As they approached the cross street Jacqueline noticed three men walking their way. She couldn't see their faces because they were each wearing a hoodie that seemed ever so popular these days. She quietly elbowed Bret to alert him. He had seen them and gestured for Jacqueline to follow him across the street.

Two of the men crossed the street almost immediately. The third man stopped walking and just waited.

Bret whispered, "Jacqueline, call 911, now—right now."

She didn't need to be told, as she was already groping through her purse for the cell. She punched 911 as she looked at the approaching men.

"Please state your emergency," said a voice on the other end of the line.

"We're on Franklin Boulevard between Holmes and Jefferson. I believe we are about to be attacked by three men wearing hoodies."

"I am sending a patrol car right away. Is there anywhere you can get to safely?"

Jacqueline stopped speaking. One of the men pulled out a knife and angled it like he was very confident about how to use it.

Bret put his hands up in the air. "Look man, we don't want any trouble. Nothing in my wallet is that important to me. Take it, there's at least two hundred dollars in it." He started reaching for his wallet but held on to it as he turned to Jacqueline.

He looked at Jacqueline and said, "Throw your purse down so these men can take what they want."

Jacqueline didn't think these men would be satisfied with their money. She had this funny feeling they wanted something more.

One of the men spoke directly to Bret. "We want Jacqueline. If you wish to live, walk away now."

Bret looked over at Jacqueline like he was actually considering the notion. Jacqueline couldn't believe it. She always knew deep down that Bret could not be counted on when he was really needed.

As if reading her mind, knowing that she thought he was a low down dirty dog, he rallied at the last second.

"See here. You can't accost us. The police are on their way."

The second man pulled out a weapon of some kind. It sort of looked like a flashlight to Jacqueline but it was kind of skinny in the middle. He pointed it toward Bret's head.

He screamed, "Sorry Jacqueline, I can't do this." He started backing away slowly as the two men looked on smiling. Bret turned on his heels and ran down the street.

Jacqueline was flabbergasted that he had actually left her alone with these thugs. As the men slowly advanced on her, she retreated backwards for each step they took forward. She still had her purse. She carefully felt around in her purse until she securely put her fingers around what she had been searching for.

The two men rushed forward. Jacqueline pulled out her mace and sprayed the men as they tried to grab her. They both put their hands over their eyes, as they started to scream from the pain. The third man, however, was now crossing the street when they all heard the siren of the approaching police car as it turned onto Franklin Boulevard. The man that had now crossed the street decided to give up his pursuit. Instead, he pushed the other two men toward a waiting van that appeared. All three men jumped into the van and disappeared down the street.

Seconds later a police car pulled up to the curb beside Jacqueline. A police officer got out. After ascertaining no one was injured and nothing was stolen, the officer posed a series of questions for Jacqueline to answer. Twenty minutes later, an officer drove Jacqueline to her car. The officer had strongly suggested that she shouldn't stay alone at her house tonight. In addition, she had suggested calling a friend. Jacqueline thanked her and promised to call someone.

A separate patrol car had searched for the van, but without an accurate license plate, their hands were tied. There were thousands of white vans in the city.

Jacqueline followed the officer's advice and texted two of her closest friends, Amber and Alicia. Neither one of her friends were home. Amber had gone to stay for a long weekend in NYC. Alicia had met up with her fiancé and together they were traveling to St. Thomas for the week.

Alicia returned her text and let her know the next door neighbor had a spare key to her place. Graciously, she had called her neighbor and prearranged for Jacqueline to pick up the spare key.

Jacqueline thanked Alicia profusely for coming to her aid, and told her she was a gem for helping her out. Quite frankly, she felt scared to go to her apartment tonight. She had tried not to dwell on the fact that three men tried to grab her. And… they knew her name. *Oh my god, what am I going to do? I will have to go back to my apartment tomorrow. How will I ever feel safe again?*

Her phone rang, it was Bret. "The no good, low down, dirty dog," she said out loud to herself. The phone continued to ring. On the third ring, she picked it up.

"Hello! What the hell do you want jerk?" snapped Jacqueline.

"Jacqueline. Thank God. I was so worried. I left for you, you know. I thought they might start a knife fight or something. I didn't go very far. I would have come back if I thought they were going to hurt you. I swear I would have."

Seething with indignation, she had to force herself to speak. "What a lying damn dog you are. I'm hanging up now. Never bother me again."

"Wait, Jacqueline. Wait. I promise you, I wouldn't have let anything bad happen to you. You, you... won't spread any negative stories about our breakup will you? I mean, everyone would think you're just being sore. You won't say anything about tonight, will you?"

Jacqueline didn't say anything. She was so incensed, so appalled; she didn't know what to say.

"Jacqueline. Are you still there?

"I'm still here, jerk."

"Please. I'm so sorry about everything tonight. I'm asking you not to tell anyone or post anything. Please."

"I'll think about it."

"Oh, thank you, Jacqueline. My job could be at stake. Please don't ruin my life. I'm so sorry, really. I wish nothing but the very best for you."

"I'm hanging up now, Bret."

"Good night. And, thanks again."

What a weasel. He made her so mad. But, it was over. She didn't want to ruin his future, even if he was someone she should let the world at large know could never be counted on. He probably had someone out there for him, or maybe he shouldn't be with anyone; in any case, he wasn't her problem anymore.

As she walked through the condo she was struck by the eclectic style and how well it all seemed to work. Alicia had a midcentury coffee table and sofa positioned near the far wall. A set of windows were encased in the exposed brick wall. She had exposed piping as well. That, along with the open concept, gave her condo an industrial loft feel that appealed to Jacqueline. An early American armoire stood near the front door with Asian vases tastefully filled with Pussy Willows on either side.

The Persian rug, with its deep rouge and sapphire silk threads, led the way down the hall where Alicia's self-portrait hung. It was quite large with a silver leaf frame that brought your eyes to the work. The artwork had special lighting, which highlighted the bold brushstrokes that evoked a feeling of being exposed.

Her face held you captive as she bared her essence and left one with questions. Did she love life, or did she mourn for someone lost to her? Her eyes drew you in and captivated your soul. For some unexplained reason, tears welled up and slowly rolled down her cheek.

Jacqueline knew her friend was a gifted artist but this work was so moving she had no doubt she was looking at a masterpiece that would one day be world famous. Why did Alicia hide this work of art in her condo? She was going to yell at her friend when she came home. She would tell her that she should have this included in her upcoming exhibition in NYC.

Her thoughts were interrupted by a loud knock at the door. Alicia's condo had a security guard in the lobby. A gentleman, Mr. Beauregard, was on duty tonight and knew Jacqueline was staying the night. Thoroughly confused as to who could possibly know she was here, Jacqueline approached the door with more and more apprehension. She looked at the visual monitor mounted beside the front door. It displayed a fairly young man smartly dressed in a suit.

Not recognizing the individual, she pushed the button to speak with the man. "Can I help you?"

The man straightened and pushed back a wealth of thick blonde hair. He looked like a model. *He must turn heads everywhere he goes*, she thought.

"Yes. Well, actually I am looking for a Miss Jacqueline Moore."

"I don't understand. Who are you, and what do you want with Miss Moore?"

"Are you Miss Moore?" questioned the man.

"Yes, but I still don't understand," replied Jacqueline.

"Miss Moore, I am Detective Upton. I need to speak with you about the incident tonight. May I come in?"

"Show me your badge." It was not a request; she had said it as more of an order. She had a funny feeling about this. Something wasn't right.

He raised his badge to the camera. She stood there holding her hand in mid-air resisting the urge to open the door. *What is wrong with me, I'm letting tonight get to me. No one wants to grab me—I'm just an interior designer.*

"Miss Moore, are you still there?"

"Yes, I'm sorry."

Ignoring her intuition, she opened the door and moved to the side to allow the officer entry. He moved into the room and looked Jacqueline over.

"Are you okay, Miss Moore?"

"Yes, fine. I'm sorry for my rudeness, I guess tonight has shook me up more than I realized."

"I understand completely," replied Detective Upton.

"Please take a seat."

Jacqueline motioned for Detective Upton to follow her lead. She walked over to the sofa and sat down rather abruptly. She felt drained emotionally and physically. She needed a long hot shower and a nice warm bed.

Detective Upton took his cue and followed her. He chose the chair and ottoman instead.

"May I inquire how you are doing? You look like you need to lie down."

"I'm fine, really. How can I help you?"

"The officer at the scene neglected to collect some important information."

"Oh, what would that be?" questioned Jacqueline. She was beginning to feel uncomfortable with the situation but unsure what to do; he was a detective after all.

He reached into the breast pocket of his jacket and pulled out a rather large piece of cloth. At first glance it looked like a handkerchief. Jacqueline thought he needed to blow his nose.

He walked over to the sofa. He stated, "We found this at the scene. I was wondering if you recognize this embellishment."

He walked over and held out the cloth for closer inspection. It was white with blue and green swirls surrounding a pattern of numbers of various sizes. She remembered thinking it strange that a Detective would go to all this trouble just to question her knowledge of this cloth. It made no sense.

She remembered struggling with Detective Upton. He put the cloth over her mouth from behind. At first, she tried to jump up off the sofa but one hand was firmly over her face with the other on her shoulder, forcing her back down.

Her thoughts were racing. Why was he doing this? Who was he? She didn't think he could be a detective, not really. Things were becoming a little fuzzy. Knowing she was mixing up thoughts while mumbling through the cloth, which only caused her to inhale the noxious odor more, she couldn't formulate a plan of action. She would, formulate a plan, that is, as soon as she rested a minute or two. No. No resting. It was important not to rest just now.

She seemed overly tired for some reason. Was it time to go to work yet? Maybe she should just stop fighting. Why was she fighting taking a rest? Nothing was making sense right now.

He kept telling her softly in her ear, "Stop fighting me, Jacqueline. You won't win this one. Just lay back and rest. Everything is going to be fine, Jacqueline. You are getting sleepy now. Close your eyes for me, Jacqueline."

The rest was just words slurred together; she couldn't understand any of this. She would just lie back against the sofa for just a second or two. *Focus Jacqueline, focus. What is wrong with me?*

A special thanks to my readers. I have dreamed of being an author for many years now. Inspired by writers before me, I took the plunge—but without you, the reader, my dreams would be just that— dreams. ~ Jackie Mae

Please connect with me:

 Like me on Facebook at:
www.facebook.com/AuthorJackieMae

Follow me on Twitter at:
www.twitter.com/@jackiemaeauthor

Contact Information:

Email: jackiemaebooks@gmail.com

Website: www.jackiemae.com